MEGHADŪTAM

AF888762

Maghadūtam

By Mahakavi Kalidas

Translated by

Amb. Dr. Prakash Joshi

MOTILAL BANARSIDASS INTERNATIONAL
DELHI

First Edition : Delhi, 2024

© Author
All Rights Reserved

ISBN : 978-81-19394-38-8

Also available at

MOTILAL BANARSIDASS INTERNATIONAL
H. O.- 41 U.A. Bungalow Road, (Back Lane)Jawahar Nagar, Delhi - 110 007
4261 (basement) Lane #3,Ansari Road, Darya Ganj, New Delhi - 110 002
203 Royapettah High Road, Mylapore, Chennai - 600 004
12/1A, 2nd Floor, Bankim Chatterjee Street, Kolkata - 700 073
Stockist : Motilal Books, Ashok Rajpath, Near Kali Mandir, Patna - 800 004

No part of this book may be reproduced in any form or by any electronic or mechanical means including information storage and retrieval systems without permission in writing from the publishers, excepts by a reviewer who may quote brief passages in a review.

Printed in India
MOTILAL BANARSIDASS INTERNATIONAL

CONTENTS

Author's Foreword

It indeed gives me great pleasure to write these few words as a foreword to my English translation of Mahākavi Kalidas' seminal lyric 'Meghadūtam'. While presenting this translation in its finished format to esteemed readers, as I look back, I cannot but recall that this indeed has been a long, long trek involving much editing and reediting.

It has been truly a labour of love but such is the fantastic beauty of Meghadūtam that it never jades, there is never a sense of deja vu, no matter how many times you read it. In this sense Meghadūtam like other great literary works is immortal.

Meghadūtam ranks only next to Śakuntalam in Mahākavi Kalidas' liteary corpus. It represents wailings of an anguished husband desperately trying to get in touch with his beloved wife who is far, far away. It is essentially a saga of love and is certainly second to none in the sheer sublimity of its language.

The reader may wonder why I have attempted a translation of "Meghadūtam", admittedly no easy task, when there have been other translations. It would be pertinent to point out here that all translations are not one and the same; the sensibilities, the linguistic inclinations, and above all translator's own unique understanding of the subject matter ensure that the translation done by him gets set apart from previous translations by a certain novelty and originality.

While translating Sanskrit classics like Meghadūtam, I am always guided by certain principles. First, every effort is made to ensure that the translation precisely conforms to the original text. All extra words added for elucidation are always put in brackets. The syntax of the original text, including the widely used passive tense in Sanskrit, is retained in the translation as far as possible. However, and this is most important, no effort is spared to ensure that the translation rolls out smoothly and captures to some extent at least the charm and elegance of the original text.

Having said all this, let me briefly explain the theme of Meghdūtam.

The narrative begins with the description of a certain Yakśa who had committed some infraction. He was expelled by Kubera from the Alakāpurī, his fabled city of unimaginable wealth, and asked to go to the earth. Accordingly the Yakśa takes up his residence on the top of the Rāmgiri mountain in central India.

कश्चित्कान्ताविरहगुरुणा स्वाधिकारात्प्रमत्त:
शापेनास्तंगमितमहिमा वर्षभोग्येण भर्तुः।
यक्षश्चक्रे जनकतनयास्नानपुण्योदकेषु
स्निग्धच्छायातरुषु वसतिं रामगिर्याश्रमेषु ।। १ ।।

Purvardh a Verse No. 1:

"A certain Yakśa[1]*, remiss in his duties,*
Bearing (hence) the curse of (his) Lord (Kubera),
To be suffered year long,
Unendurable due to separation from (his) beloved wife;
(The Yakśa) whose (divine) powers had faded away,
Thanks to the curse,
Had made (his) abode,
Among the hermitages of Rāmgiri[2]*,*
Under delightfully thick shade of trees,
(And) whose waters were sacred,
Being bathed in,
By the daughter of (king) Janaka, Sitādevi[3]*."*

---

[1] Yakśās as per mythology are the attendants of Kubera, the Lord of wealth. They are demigods and hence deemed worthy of reverence. The name of this Yakśa has not been given in this lyric anywhere. This could be due to the norm that in holy texts names of those who flout the orders of their masters should not be mentioned. It is noteworthy in this lyric Mahākavi Kālidās has directly introduced the subject while in his other works he usually begins with a salutation to God or a benediction.

[2] Rāmgiri connotes the "mountain of Lord Rāma". The mountain is so named because Lord Rāma reputedly lived there for some time along with Laxman and Sitāji during their exile. It is identified by some with Chitrakuta in Bundelkhand.

The hapless Yakśa is extremely grieved being separated from his beloved wife. Suddenly, he espies a cloud at the top of the Rāmgiri mountain. A thought then comes to the mind of Yakśa: "Why not send a message to his wife through the medium of the cloud."

संतप्तानां त्वमसि शरणं तत्पयोद प्रियाया:
संदेशं मे हर धनपतिक्रोधविश्लेषितस्य ।
गन्तव्या ते वसतिरलका नाम यक्षेश्वराणां
बाह्योद्यानस्थितहरशिरश्चन्द्रिकाधौतहर्म्या ।। ७ ।।

Purvardha Verse No. 7:

"Oh Cloud ! you are the refuge of the distressed[4]*,*
So bear my message,
To my beloved,
Separated as I am (from her),
By the wrath of the Lord of Wealth,
(The Kubera);
The abode of the Lords[5] *of Yakśās (Kubera),*
Named as Alakā,[6]
Being your destination;
Its mansions being illumined by rays of the moon,
Ensconced on the head of Śivaji,
Residing in the garden outside (Alakā)"

Thus begins the epic journey of the Cloud from central India to Alkāpurī on the Kailāś mountain. In this narrative the Cloud (Megha) acts as an intermediary between the Yakśa and his beloved wife. This is how the text came to be named 'Meghdūtam'.

---

[3] Dev. Sitā is believed to have taken a bath in the waters of Rāmgiri sanctifying them.
[4] The Cloud is so depicted as it gives relief to those suffering from the heat of summer.
[5] The plural term 'Lords' is used in an honorific way for Kubera.
[6] This is the capital of Kubera renowned for its unimaginable wealth.

The Yakśa then goes on to lay out the path which the Cloud should follow to reach Alkāpurī. This is what the first part of the text or 'Purvardha' is about. It is essentially a travelogue in which there is a detailed description of rivers, mountains, etc., which the Cloud will pass over as he traverses from the Rāmgiri mountain to the fabled Kailaś mountain. Most notably many of these names bear a close resemblance, if not being identical, to those used in modern times.

There is a fantastic depiction of Ujjayini.

पत्रश्यामा दिनकरहयस्पर्धिनो यत्र वाहाः
शैलोदग्रास्त्वमिव करिणो वृष्टिमन्तः प्रभेदात् ।
योधाग्रण्यः प्रतिदशमुखं संयुगे तस्थिवान्सः
प्रत्यादिष्टाभरणरुचयश्चन्द्रहासव्रणाङ्कैः ।। ३५ ।।

Purvardha Verse No. 35:

"Where (in Ujjayini) are horses,
Greenish dark like leaves,
Rivalling the sun's steads;
Mountain (like) towering elephants,
Ichor streaming out,[7]
Showering rains,
Resembling yourself;
(Its) leading warriors having steadfastly faced,
Rāvana in battle[8]*;*
Have abandoned (their) love of ornaments,
Thanks to the marks of scars,
Made by Rāvana's sword"

[7] This is how huge, powerful elephants of that era were customarily portrayed in the Sanskrit literature.

[8] Ujjayini is described as having been wrenched away from the heaven (see verse no. 31 in the Purvardha in the main text). Rāvana had once tried to carry off the Kailāś mountain to Lankā as he was a supreme devotee of Śivaji. (See verse 62). A battle had then ensued. This is how probably in the imagination of the Mahākavi warriors of Ujjayini which was then a part of heaven and therefore of Kailāś confronted Rāvana in battle.

The famous Mahakala temple finds mention as follows.

अप्यन्यस्मिन् जलधर महाकालमासाद्य काले
स्थातव्यं ते नयनविषयं यावदत्येति भानुः ।
कुर्वन्सन्ध्यावलिपटहतां शूलिनः श्लाघनीया-
मामन्द्राणां फलमविकलं लप्स्यसे गर्जितानाम् ।। ३८ ।।

Purvardha Verse No. 38:

"Oh ! Cloud (Carrier of water),
Even if the (shrine) of Mahākāla[9]*,*
Was to be reached (by you),
During some period (other than evening),
Remain there,
Until the sun vanishes,
From your eyesight;
You will (then) gain,
The reward in entirety,
Of (your) staid thunderings[10]*,*
Having played the commendable role,
Of producing the sounds of Pataha (a big drum),[11]
During the evening worship of Śivaji"

At the end of Purvardha the Cloud reaches Alkāpurī, his destination.

तस्योत्सङ्गे प्रणयिन इव स्त्रस्तगङ्गादुकूलां
न त्वं दृष्ट्वा न पुनरलकां ज्ञास्यसे कामचारिन् ।
या वः काले वहति सलिलोद्गारमुच्चैर्विमाना
मुक्ताजालग्रथितमलकं कामिनीवाभ्रवृन्दम् ।।६७।।

[9] Notably to present times the Mahākāla temple remains one of the most sacred shrines in India, especially of Śivaji.
[10] The Mahākavi by the phrase 'staid thundering' probably wishes to convey rumbling of moderate intensity in a steady and not haphazard way.
[11] The evening worship of Śivaji is regarded as the most significant among his three daily Āaratis. A percussion instrument with distinctive notes called 'Nagādā' is played at this time even in present times. This percussion instrument was probably called 'Pataha' in Mahākavi's times. This brings out the continuity of ritualistic traditions in India.

Purvardha Verse No. 67:

"Marked by towering mansions,
The Alakā (Nagari) [12],
(Nestles) in the lap of that lover (of hers),
(The Kailāś mountain);
The Ganges river,
Being as if (her) (Alakā Nagarī's)
White silken upper garment,[13]
That has slipped down;
In your (favourite) season, Oh ! Free-Wanderer, (Oh ! Cloud),
(In the monsoon),
(The Alakā Nagari) which bears multitudes of clouds,
Spewing water,
Resembling a gentle and serene damsel,
(Her) hair interwoven with pearl-strings[14]*;*
Having seen (once) the Alakā (Nagarī),
No way can you then,
Not know it"

In the second part or the 'Uttaradha' the Cloud is guided to Yakśa's residence where his beloved wife is residing and advised as to how he should address her so as not to discomfit her by his sudden appearance.

Alkāpurī is truly a fabulous place where everyone is blissfully happy, where flowers of all seasons perpetually bloom and where passionate and unrestrained sensuous pleasures find their fullest expression.

यत्रोन्मत्तभ्रमरमुखराः पादपा नित्यपुष्पाः,

---

[12] Alakā is the fabled capital city of Kubera.

[13] Alakā is situated on the top of the Kailāś mountain. The Ganges with her sparkling white waters flows below. This is why a simile is drawn by the Mahākavi between the Ganges and a silken white upper garment of the beloved maiden that has dropped off.

[14] The pearl-strings correspond to rain waters while the dark clouds resemble the tresses.

हंसश्रेणीरचितरशना नित्यपद्मा नलिन्यः ।
केकोत्कण्ठा भवनशिखिनो नित्यभास्वत्कलापा
नित्यज्योत्स्ना प्रतिहततमोवृत्तिरम्याः प्रदोषाः ।।३।।

Uttaradha Verse No. 3:

"Wherein (in the Alakā city),
The trees there being ever flower bearing,
Noisy due to (humming) of bees,
Gone amuck;
Lakes with lotuses always blooming,
Rings of swans,
Arrayed (around them),
(Like) waistbands;
Domesticated peacocks (their) plumages ever radiant,
(Sweetly) cooing,
Being upraised of necks;
Delightful being the nights,
The envelope of darkness dissipated,
With the moon light eternally present"

The inhabitants of Alkāpurī indulged themselves in every possible way. The following stanza illustrates their uninhibited lifestyle.

नीवीबन्धोच्छ्वसितशिथिलं यत्र बिम्बाधराणाम्
क्षौमं रागादनिभृतकरेष्वाक्षिपत्सु प्रियेषु ।
अर्चिस्तुङ्गानभिमुखमपि प्राप्य रत्नप्रदीपान्
ह्रीमूढानां भवति विफलप्रेरणा चूर्णमुष्टिः ।।७।।

Uttaradha Verse No. 7:

"Where (in that city of Alakā),
As the lovers with restless hands,
Overwhelmed by passion,
Rip off the silk inner garment,
Being loose its knots unravelled,
Of (their beloved ladies);

With 'bimba' (like) lower lip,[15]
They turning witless out of modesty,[16]
(Fling fistful of powder,
Towards jewel-lamps);
(But) futile proves (their) effort,[17]
(Despite)(that) powder reaching the jewel-lamps,
Its rays of light shooting up"[18]

The Yakśini, the Yakśa's wife, is characterized as the most beautiful woman in the world.

तन्वी श्यामा शिखरिदशना पक्वबिम्बाधरोष्ठी
मध्ये क्षामा चकितहरिणीप्रेक्षणा निम्ननाभिः ।
श्रोणीभारादलसगमना स्तोकनम्रा स्तनाभ्याम्,
या तत्र स्याद्युवतिविषये सृष्टिराद्येव धातुः ।।२२।।

Uttaradha Verse No. 22:

"(Describing the appearance of his wife,
The Yakśa narrates),[19]
The damsel who would be there,
(In my mansion),
Being youthful and slim,
With pointed teeth,[20]
Lower lip (like) a ripe bimba (fruit),[21]
Slender in the middle,

---

[15] The bimba is a red fruit. This simile is usually used to describe the lips of a beautiful lady.

[16] The Mahākavi shows familiarity with female psychology which has presumably not changed over the centuries.

[17] The lamps were enkindled by gems. This is why dust could not extinguish them as would have happened in case of ordinary oil lamps. This shows that the gems in the Alakā city had amazing radiance and sparkle.

[18] --ibid--

[19] The Yakśa had earlier depicted the prominent features of his palace so that the Cloud could easily locate it. Next he elaborates his wife's charming looks so that she could be identified by the Cloud.

[20] Married ladies (with pointed teeth) were considered fortunate for their husbands.

[21] Widely used simile in Sanskrit literature for the portrayal of a beautiful damsel.

Eyes (like) a startled doe,[22]
Deep of naval,[23]
Slow of gait due to heaviness of hips,[24]
Learning forward a little,
Due to (expansive) breasts;[25]
As if she happens to be,[26]
The very first creation,
Among the female species
Of the creator"

The Yakśa missing his wife immeasurably longs intensely for her and even while dreaming only thinks of his beloved.

मामाकाशप्रणिहितभुजं निर्दयाश्लेषहेतो-
लब्धायास्ते कथमपि मया स्वप्नसंदर्शनेषु ।
पश्यन्तीनां न खलु बहुशो न स्थलीदेवतानां
मुक्तास्थूलास्तरुकिसलयेष्वश्रुलेशाः पतन्ति ।।४६।।

Uttaradha Verse No. 46:

"Somehow or other in a dream vision,
Myself[27] *having got hold of you*[28]*,*
With a view to tightly embracing you;
Forest deities observing me[29]*,*
Arms extended in space,
Usually (then) come down as a matter of course,
(Their) tear drops, large (like) pearls,
On plant leaves"

---

22 --ibid--
23 These show how the criteria and benchmarks of female beauty have changed over the centuries.
24 --ibid--
25 --ibid--
26 This damsel is none but Yakśa's wife.
27 Refers to the Yakśa. He continues to narrate his message meant for his wife to the Cloud.
28 This connotes the Yakśiṇi.
29 The Yakśa is referred.

Finally, the lyric ends with the Yakśa expressing the pious hope that the Cloud after delivering his message to the Yakṣiṇi would return to him soonest possible, thus sustaining his life. He also expresses his fervent wish that the Cloud would not be separated from his beloved (the lightning) as the Yakśa was.

एतत्कृत्वा प्रियमनुचितप्रार्थनावर्तिनो मे
सौहर्दाद् वा विधुर इति वा मय्यनुक्रोशबुद्ध्या ।
इष्टान् देशान् जलद ! विचर प्रावृषा संभृतश्री-
र्मा भूदेवं क्षणमपि च ते विद्युता विप्रयोगः ॥५५॥

Uttaradha Verse No. 55:
"Either out of friendship,
Or sense of pity for me,[30]
Being separated (from the beloved),
Having accomplished this (mission),[31]
Dear to me,
(Despite) myself putting forth an improper solicitation;[32]
Wander off, Oh ! Cloud,
Over wonderful regions,
(Your) glory enhanced by the rainy season;
And may there not be,
Even momentarily your separation,
From the lightning,
Like this,
(As happened in my case)[33] "

The Meghadūtam is a saga of intense passionate love and of the pathos of separation - these themes are common in all the dramas of the Mahākavi. It is also a travelogue covering vast tracts of

---

[30] Refers to the Yakśa.
[31] Connotes the Cloud successfully delivering the Yakśa's message to his wife.
[32] As explained in stanza no. 5 in the Purvardha the Cloud was hardly regarded as an appropriate messenger for carrying the message of love.
[33] The lightning and the Cloud are deemed as the eternal pair of lovers. Yakśa evidently did not want the Cloud to suffer from pangs of separation even momentarily as he had done.

India and its description of rivers, mountains, etc. corresponds to the topography of the land as we know it. This clearly betokens the thread of continuity running through the Indian civilization during the last two millennia. The hedonistic pleasures of wealthy Yakśas in Alkāpuri are portrayed in minute detail. There are explicit depictions of love-making bordering on eroticism along with repeated allusions to mythology and folklore. All this is couched in the exquisitely incomparable idioms and expressions of the Mahākavi which makes this text an unending feast to the eyes and mind.

Finally, in the end it is my pleasant duty to express my heartfelt thanks to all those who made completion of this project possible.

First of all, let me record my profound thanks to Professor Dr. Arknath Choudhary, former Vice-Chancellor of Sri Somanath Sanskrit University, for his constant support and encouragement. His translation and commentary on Meghadūtam has been my Bible and my translation closely follows the "Bhavarth" in Sanskrit as given by him. At my specific request he has been good enough to write a preface for this publication in chaste Sanskrit.

I am also grateful to Professor Dr.Radha Vallabh Tripathi, former Head of the Central Sanskrit University, New Delhi, and a foremost scholar of Sanskrit and Indology, who found time in his busy schedule to go through my translation more than once and made several suggestions towards its improvement. Needless to say all of them have been duly incorporated. He has also been gracious enough to append his preface to this publication.

I am also grateful to Shri Deepak Jain of New Bharatiya Book Corporation for readily agreeing to publish this book. He is engaged in the admittedly difficult task of publishing and promoting high-quality books dealing with Sanskrit, Indology, etc. I wish him all luck in this endeavour.

My sincere thanks are also due to Vandanaji Eksambekar of Asmita Enterprises, Pune, who over the last many years has been painstakingly typing my manuscripts. Her role in the completion of this project is no way insignificant.

Finally, I must record my deep appreciation of my wife Nalini who has always stood by me and supported my literary and spiritual pursuits.

With these few words, seeking Devi Saraswati's blessings and grace I lay this book in the hands of the reader. It is my sincere hope that the perusal of this translation would help him to savour the elegance and the charm of Mahākavi's writings. If this happens, my labour would be amply rewarded.

प्रो. अर्कनाथ चौधरी

(पूर्व कुलपति. श्री सोमनाथ संस्कृत विश्वविद्यालय. गुजरात सरकार,

पूर्व निदेशक, केन्द्रीय संस्कृत विश्वविद्यालय, जयपुर, मुम्बई, लखनऊ परिसर)

दि. **23/08/2022**

अप्रतिमगीतिकाव्यं मेघदूतम्

संसारस्य प्राचीनतमकृतिं वेदं वेदादिसम्बद्धसाहित्यञ्चारभ्य लौकिकसंस्कृतसाहित्यं यावत् समग्रमपि संस्कृतवाङ्मयं भारतीयसंस्कृतेरजस्रं स्रोतो वर्तते। भारतीयसंस्कृतेः प्राणतत्वं खलु आध्यात्मिकचैतन्यं,तेन संस्कृतसाहित्यं परिपूर्णम्। अस्मिन् साहित्ये तपस्त्यागवैराग्यदयौदार्यसहानुभूतिदानोपासनादीनां चर्चया सह लोककल्याणविशिष्टभावानां च उल्लेखः बाहुल्येन कृतो विद्यते। एते च विलक्षणाः भावा वाल्मीकिव्यासभासकालिदासाश्वघोषभारविभवभूतिश्रीहर्ष- दण्डीमाघबाणप्रभृतीनां महाकवीनां रचनासु कान्तासम्मितोपदेशेन सह सन्ति गुम्फिताः।

अतिविशालस्य लौकिकसाहित्यस्य महत्त्वपूर्णो भागः काव्यसाहित्यम्। काव्यसाहित्यं दृश्यश्रव्यभेदेन द्विधा। साहित्य दर्पणे विश्वनाथेन प्रोक्तम्- **'दृश्यश्रव्यत्वभेदेन पुनः काव्यं द्विधा मतम्। दृश्यं तत्राभिनेयं स्याद्रूपारोपात्तु रूपकम्'** इति। महाकविः कालिदासः उभयविधरचनयोः कृते समग्रे विश्वे ख्याततमः। अत एवायं विश्वकविरपि कथ्यते। कालिदासस्य दृश्यकाव्येषु अभिज्ञानशाकुन्तलम्, विक्रमोर्वशीयम्,मालविकाग्निमित्रं च। रघुवंशं कुमारसंभवं मेघदूतम् ऋतुसंहारश्च। रघुवंशं कुमारसंभवं च महाकाव्यम् ऐतिहासिकं पौराणिकश्चेतिवृत्तमादाय विन्यस्तम्। कवेः प्रथमं काव्यम् ऋतुवर्णनपरकम् ऋतुसंहारः। विप्रलम्भशृङ्गारस्य अत्यन्तमद्भुतं लोकहृदयरञ्जकं प्रकृतिपुरुषयोः वैशिष्ट्यदर्शकं मेघदूतम् 'गीतिकाव्यं' खण्डकाव्यं वा मन्यते आलङ्कारिकैः।

अप्रतिमं गीतिकाव्यं मेघदूतम्-

स्वकर्तव्यपालनात् च्युतः कश्चित् यक्षः स्वामिना कुबेरेण वर्षभोग्येण निष्कासनदण्डेन दण्डितः सन् रामगिरि- नामक- पर्वते वर्तमाने रामटेक इति नाम्ना ख्याते निवसति। वर्षर्तोः प्रथमस्य मासस्य आषाढस्य प्रथमे दिवसे पर्वतशिखरारूढं वप्रक्रीडापरिणत गज इव दर्शनीयं मेघं विलोक्य असह्यविरहवेदनया पीडितः कामार्तो यक्षः प्रियतमां प्रति स्वजीवितस्य संदेशं प्रेषयितुं मेघं समर्च्य दौत्यकर्मणे प्रार्थयति। अतः अस्य काव्यस्य- मेघः दूतं यस्मिन्, तत्, अथवा मेघश्चासौ दूतः मेघदूतः, तमधिकृत्य कृतं काव्यं 'मेघदूतम्' इति नाम कृतम्। दौत्यं चेतनस्य कार्यम्, अचेतनो मेघः कथङ्कारं दौत्यं कुर्वीत इत्याक्षेपनिवारणाय स्वयं कालिदासः संदिशति- **'कामार्ता हि प्रकृतिकृपणाश्चेतनाचेतनेषु'** इति। किञ्च कामार्तस्य हि जनस्य चेतनस्य एतत्कर्म अचेतनस्य वेति विवेको न भवति। अत एव मेघं दृष्ट्वा विह्वलः सन् प्राणप्रियाजीवितालम्बनार्थी सः यक्षः धूमज्योतिःसलिलमरुतां सन्निपातम् अचेतनं मेघं दौत्यकार्याय निवेदयति। कथं न निवेदयेत्, यतो हि निवेदनस्य औचित्यमस्ति प्रबलम्, तद्धि-

'मेघालोके भवति सुखिनोऽप्यन्यथावृत्तिचेतः। कण्ठाश्लेषप्रणयिनि जने किं पुनर्दूरसंस्थे' इति।

महाकविः वाल्मीकिः रामायणे सीतान्वेषणाय वानरं दूतं कृत्वा प्रैषयत् किन्तु महाकविः कालिदासः अचेतनं मेघं दूतं नियुङ्क्ते, यश्च दूतः मेघः प्रकृतिं जीवयति, अवन्ध्यां कृत्वा तां पूर्णयति सुशोभयति च। सः सकलस्य भूमण्डलस्य जीवनदाता अवश्यं विरहाकुलस्य यक्षस्य प्रियतमायाः जीवनं रक्षिष्यति इति विशिष्टं भावमपि व्यञ्जयति। वर्णनवैशिष्ट्येन पाठका भावयन्ति यत् साक्षात् चेतनेन साकं यक्षः संवादं करोति। किञ्च दूतः बुद्धिमान् चतुरः उच्चकुले जातोऽस्ति इति वर्णनप्रसङ्गे लोकनीतिव्यवहारमपि निर्दिशति- याञ्चा मोघा वरमिति कथनेन। अर्थात् श्रेष्ठजन एव कार्यसिद्ध्यै याचनीयः न तु अधमो जनः। श्रेष्ठविषये कृता याचना व्यर्था भवति चेदपि वरम्,अधमो न याचनीयः कदापि। एतादृशं प्रकृतिसन्तर्पण-पोषण-गुणविशिष्टं श्रेष्ठं मेघं दौत्याय यक्षमुखेन विनिवेदयन् महाकविः प्रशंसति,

व्यवहारनीतिमप्युपस्थापयति तथा हि -

जातं वंशे भुवनविदिते पुष्करावर्तकानां, जानामि त्वां प्रकृतिपुरुषं कामरूपं मघोनः।
तेनार्थित्वं त्वयि विधिवशात् दूरबन्धुर्गतोऽहं, याञ्चा मोघा वरमधिगुणे नाधमे लब्धकामा॥
इति।

पुष्करावर्तकानां प्रशस्तमेघानां वंशे जातोऽयं मेघो मघवतः इच्छारूपधारी प्रकृतिपुरुषःविशिष्टगुणयुक्तः, अतः एतादृशस्य दौत्यकर्माचरणाय निवेदने अनौचित्यं नास्तीति प्रतिपादयति। अर्थान्तरन्यासस्य प्रेयोऽलङ्कारस्य वा सुप्रयोगोऽपि कृत महाकविना। किञ्च संतप्तानां शरणीभूतो मेघः अलकानगर्यां विद्यमानायै प्रियायै संदेशं नीत्वा गच्छेच्चेत् तत्र स्थितान् चराचरान् संतोशयिष्यत्यवश्यम्। प्रशंसया मेघो गर्वितो मा भूत् इति बोधनाय यादृशः कामरूपोऽपूर्वः मेघः,तादृशी एव अलकानगरी तथैव अनिन्द्यसुन्दरी यक्षप्रिया इति वर्ण्यते। तथा हि -

विद्युत्वन्तं ललितवनिताः सेन्द्रचापं सचित्राः, संगीताय प्रहतमुरजाः स्निग्धगम्भीरघोषम्।
अन्तस्तोयं मणिमयभुवस्तुङ्गमभ्रंलिहाङ्गाः, प्रासादास्त्वां तुलयितुमलं यत्र तैस्तैर्विशेषैः॥

यक्षस्य प्रिया विधातुः प्रथमा सृष्टिरिवास्ति। यथोक्तमस्मिन् पद्ये -

तन्वी श्यामा शिखरिदशना पक्वबिम्बाधरोष्ठी, मध्ये क्षामा चकितहरिणीप्रेक्षणा निम्ननाभिः।
श्रोणीभारादलसगमना स्तोकनम्रा स्तनाभ्यां, या तत्र स्याद् युवतिविषये सृष्टिराद्येव धातुः॥
इति।

एतादृशी अपूर्वलावण्या यक्षप्रिया यस्यामलकानगर्यां वसति तस्यां विद्यमानः कल्पवृक्षः नानाविधवस्त्राणि मदिरां नवनवपुष्पाणि बहुविधमाभूषणम्, रमणीनां शृङ्गारसाधनानि च कल्पनामात्रेण प्रयच्छति। अलकायां किमपि कष्टं नास्ति कस्यचिज्जनस्य। तत्र अश्रूणि प्रसन्नतायामेव निर्गच्छन्ति न तु दुखे, तापः कामाग्नेरेव, प्रणयकलहादन्यः कलहो न भवति। प्रासादानामन्तः अक्षयनिधयः सन्ति। तत्र गमनाय यश्च मार्गः, यश्च प्रदेशः,प्रदेशानां

वैशिष्ट्यं च यत् तत्सर्वं वर्णयित्वा महाकविः तस्याः तस्याः भारतभूप्रकृतेरपूर्वं चित्रणं करोति।

प्रकृतिवर्णनम् - मेघदूते दूतीकृतो धूमज्योतिःसलिलमरुतां संनिपातो मेघः प्रकृतेः अद्भुतरूपम्, सः सजीव इव सर्वत्र अनुभावितः कविना। रामगिरेः आरभ्य अलका-यात्रामार्गे आकर्षकप्रकृतिदृश्यानां चित्रं समुपस्थापयति महाकविः। पर्वतवननदीसरिताम् उपवनग्रामनगरप्रासादादीनां च रमणीयं चित्रं ललितपदावल्यां प्रस्तौति। यथा आम्रकूटस्य पर्वतस्य वर्णनं कुर्वन् वक्ति - आम्रकूटशिखरं प्राप्ते मेघे आम्रकूटः देवयुगलैः दर्शनीयामवस्थां संप्राप्तो मध्ये श्यामः शेषविस्तारे पृथिवीनायिकायाः पीतस्तन इव प्रतीयते-

छन्नोपान्तः परिणतफलद्योतिभिः काननाम्रैस्त्वय्यारूढे शिखरमचलः स्निग्धवेणीसवर्णे। नूनं यास्यत्यमरमिथुनप्रेक्षणीयामवस्थां मध्ये श्यामः स्तन इव भुवः शेषविस्तारपाण्डुः॥

अनुकूलो वायुः मेघं मन्दं मन्दं नुदति,मेघं दृष्ट्वा गर्वितश्चातको मधुरं नदति, गर्भाधानकालं मत्वा आबद्धपङ्क्तयो नयनसुभगा बलाकाः मेघं सेविष्यन्ते। विन्ध्यस्योपत्यकायां रेवानदी गजोपरि रचिता भूतिरेखा इव दृश्यते। निर्विन्ध्याया जलं नायिकाया नितम्बात् सरत् वसनमिव प्रतीयते। तटभागे स्थितं वेत्रं नदीनायिकाया हस्त इव चित्रितं वर्तते,यथा- 'तस्याः किञ्चित् करधृतमिव प्राप्तवानीरशाखम्, हृत्वा नीलं सलिलवसनं मुक्तरोधो नितम्बम्' इति। चर्मण्वत्याः जलं ग्रहीतुं नंरीभूतो मेघः भूम्याः स्थूलमध्येन्द्रहार इव चित्रितः। रत्नकान्तिसम्मिश्रणमिव आकाशे आविर्भूतेन्द्रधनुषा युक्तो मेघः प्रतिभाति। मेघस्य शोभा च गोपवेशस्य विष्णोः शोभा इव गम्यते। कैलाशस्य शिखराणि देवाङ्गनानां कृते दर्पण इव, कैलाशश्च शिवस्य अट्टहास इव वर्णितः।

"गौरीवक्त्र भ्रुकुटिरचनां या विहस्येव फेनैः। शम्भोः केशग्रहणमकरोदिन्दुलग्नोर्मिहस्ता" ॥

इत्युक्त्या गङ्गा पार्वत्याः सपत्नीव शिवकेशलग्ना पार्वतीमुपहसतीव चित्रिता। यक्षप्रियायाः शरीरसौन्दर्यं प्रकृतौ एव प्रदर्शितं महाकविना। यथा- "श्यामास्वाङ्गं चकितहरिणी प्रेक्षणे दृष्टिपातम्" इति। कल्पवृक्षः स्त्रीणां नानाविध मण्डनानि यथा-नानावर्णं वस्त्रं, नेत्रयोः विभ्रमजनकं मधु,किसलयैः सह कुसुमविकासं,लाक्षारागादिकं च जनयति।

वासश्चित्रं मधु नयनयोर्विभ्रमादेशदक्षं , पुष्पोद्भेदं सह किसलयैर्भूषणानां विकल्पान्। लाक्षारागं चरणकमलन्यासयोग्यं च यस्यामेकः सूते सकलमबलामण्डनं कल्पवृक्षः॥

वननदीवृक्षनगरोद्यानपक्षिपशु-इन्द्रधनुषादिहृदयहारिप्रकृतिसौन्दर्यचित्रणं कालिदासेन अतिनैपुण्येन कृतम्।

मेघदूतस्य सूक्तिबाहुल्यपरकचिन्तनपूर्णार्थव्यञ्जकवचनान्यधुनाऽपि लोके प्रयुज्यन्ते। यथा- 'याच्ञा मोघा वरमधिगुणे नाधमे लब्धकामा'। 'रिक्तः सर्वो भवति हि लघुः पूर्णता गौरवाय'। 'कामार्ता हि प्रकृतिकृपणाश्चेतनाचेतनेषु'। 'मन्दायन्ते न खलु सुहृदामभ्युपेतार्थकृत्याः'। 'आपन्नार्तिप्रशमनफलाः सम्पदो ह्युत्तमानाम्'। सूर्यापाये न खलु कमलं पुष्यति स्वामभिख्याम्'। 'प्रायः सर्वो भवति करुणावृत्तिरार्द्रान्तरात्मा'। 'कस्यात्यन्तं सुखमुपनतं दुःखमेकान्ततो वा। नीचैर्गच्छत्युपरि च दशा चक्रनेमिक्रमेण'॥

महाकविकालिदासविरचितानि कव्यनाटकानि समग्रेऽपि विश्वे समादृतानि सन्ति। तत्रापि मेघदूतम् अत्यन्तं हृदयाह्लादकं गीतिकाव्यम्। सहृदयेभ्यः रोचतेतरामिदम्। अत एवोक्तं समालोचकैः- 'माघे मेघे गतं वयः' इति। विश्वमनीषा कालिदासकाव्यानि आद्रियते, अतः नैकासु विश्वभाषासु अनुवादो विहितः काव्यानाम्।

कालिदासकाव्यैः भृशं प्रभाविताः श्री प्रकाश जोशी महोदयाः विश्वस्य सहृदयबौद्धिकसमाजे कालिदासरचनावैशिष्ट्यं प्रसारयितुं अंग्रेजीभाषायां मेघदूतस्य अनुवादं कृतवन्तः, मालविकाग्निमित्रस्य विक्रमोर्वशीयस्य ऋतुसंहारस्य चापि अनुवादं कुर्वन्तः सन्ति।समये समये तैः प्रेषितोऽनुवादो मया व्यलोकि। पूर्वं मुद्राराक्षसं आंग्लानुवादसहितं श्रीसोमनाथसंस्कृतविश्वविद्यालयेन प्रकाशितम्। संस्कृतेतरक्षेत्रस्य पूर्ववैदेशिकसेवाधिकारिणः श्री प्रकाश जोशीमहोदयाः चतुष्पञ्चभिर्वर्षैः संस्कृतभाषायां नैपुण्यं प्राप्य महाकवेः काव्यानि विश्वजनीनानि कर्तुं निरन्तरं कार्यं कुर्वाणाः भारतीयसंस्कृतेः प्राक्तनभारतीयलोकजीवनस्य च समृद्धिं विज्ञापयितुं कृतनिश्चया अस्माकं प्रेरणाप्रदाः सन्ति। जोशिमहोदयानाम् अनुवादवैशिष्ट्यं प्रशंशनीयं,तेषां संस्कृतसाहित्यसेवा चापि स्तुत्या विद्यते।

श्रीप्रकाश जोशिमहोदयाः स्वस्थाः दीर्घजीविनः सन्तः निरन्तरं संस्कृतसाहित्यानुशीलने तेषां प्रकाशने च संलग्ना सन्तः संस्कृतसाहित्यं समृद्धतमं कुर्वन्तः यशस्विनः भवन्तु शिवप्रसादेन इति शम्।

(पूर्वकुलपतिः, श्रीसोमनाथ संस्कृत युनिवर्सिटी, निदेशकः, केन्द्रीय संस्कृत विश्वविद्यालयः,जयपुरपरिसरः)

Preface

A Classic transcends the barriers of time and space. It unfolds multiple readings and provides scope for manifold voices. Commentaries and Translations play a positive role for sustenance and cultivation of these readings and voices of classics from the library of world literature. Meghadūta of Kālidāsa is one of the most appropriate examples of such a classic. After Śrīmadbhagavadgītā, it is has been subjected to biggest number of commentaries (ṭīkās). Also there are hundreds of translations of this memorable poem in all the major languages of world. In fact, classics like Meghadūta not only pose a great challenge to a translator, they also invoke and invite the creativity of a person given to bi-lingual literary activity and to have an engagement with them as translator.

Creative faculty (Pratibhā) is a desideratum for the making of a good translation of a literary work. Pratibhā is said to be of two types – kārayitrī and bhāvayitrī. The former, the kārayitrī pratibhā, leads to mellifluous outburst of emotions, thoughts and ideas of an author in some form. This form is imbued with perfect aesthetic structures created by the fusion of the beauty of the sound and the sense. The second type of pratibhā, i.e., the bhāvayitrī, makes a person capable of appreciating a poem. It is by having the bhāvayitrī pratibhā that one becomes a Rasika or a Sahṛdaya. The ācāryas of literary criticism in Sanskrit (Alaṅkāraśāstra) say that the presence of both types of these pratibhās in one person is very rare. Rājaśekhara a well-known critic of X century has given an extensive treatment to the concept of pratibhā in his Kāvyamīmāṃsā. He also suggests that only some gifted sons of Sarasvatī have this rare combination of the types of pratibhās. In support of his statement, Rājaśekhara hascited the following stanza of Kālidāsa–

कश्चिद्वाचं रचयितुमलं श्रोतुमेवापरस्तां
कल्याणी ते मतिरुभयथा विस्मयं नस्तनोति ।
नह्येकस्मिन्नतिशयवतां सन्निपातो गुणाना-
मेकः सूते कनकमुपलस्तत्परीक्षाक्षमोऽन्यः।।

Here Kālidāsa is appreciating the double creative faculty of someone. The stanza says – There are some who are perfect in creating a literary piece, there are others who are given to listening it (they can appreciate it). Your acumen is so delighting, it functions on both the levels – creating and appreciating. It makes us wonder-struck, because one does not have this kind of combination of both the faculties. There is a stone (in the goldmine) which produces gold, and there is a stone (the whetstone) which testifies its purity.

The basic requirement to be a good translator is being equipped with both types of pratibhās – the kārayitrī and the bhāvayitrī. The present translation of Meghdūta by Shri P.V. Joshi stands this nikaśa -- the real test. As a connoisseur, a rasika, he has captured the spirit and the essence of Kālidāsa's poetry; and as a translator he has exhibited a rare acumen for creativity. The present translation by him satisfies a long-felt need of a good English translation of Meghadūta. Though the English translations of Meghdūta by Chandra Rajan, N.P. Unni, Datt Dinesh Chandra and various others authors are there, Joshi's translation has surpassed them all. It displays creative faculty of re-capturing Kālidāda's beauty by rendering it faithfully in a foreign language. Joshi has taken pains to consult commentaries in Sanskrit and explore alternatives to make himself a close companion of Kālidāsa.

This translation also satisfies the modern notion of a good translation. Translation is now-a-days defined as 'the replacement of a textual material in one language by equivalent textual material in another language' (Catford, J.C., 1965, A Linguistic Theory of Translation) and it 'consists in producing in receptor language the closest, natural equivalent to the message of source language, first in meaning and secondly in style (Nida, E.A., 1964, Towards Science of Translation).

Shri Joshi has really done a commendable job after painstaking studies and researches, as well as after having true bhāvanā of Kālidāsa's poem. He has made an attempt to produce the closest and most natural equivalent to Kālidāsa's poem to create a match for it in English. His translation is succinct by the way of becoming the nearest creative approximation of the original and it provides a fascinating study in Kālidāsa as well. I hope that it will be welcomed by all the lovers of poetry and the seekers of the beauties of World classics.

- Radhavallabh Tripathi

The Meghadūtam
Pūrwārdh

कश्चित्कान्ताविरहगुरुणा स्वाधिकारात्प्रमत्तः
    शापेनास्तंगमितमहिमा वर्षभोग्येण भर्तुः।
यक्षश्चक्रे जनकतनयास्नानपुण्योदकेषु
    स्निग्धच्छायातरुषु वसतिं रामगिर्याश्रमेषु ।। १ ।।

Verse No. 1:

"A certain Yakśa[1], remiss in his duties,
Bearing (hence) the curse of (his) Lord (Kubera),
To be suffered year long,
Unendurable due to separation from (his) beloved wife;
(The Yakśa) whose (divine) powers had faded away,
Thanks to the curse,
Had made (his) abode,
Among the hermitages of Rāmgiri[2],
Under delightfully thick shade of trees,
(And) whose waters were sacred,
Being bathed in,
By the daughter of (king) Janaka, Sitādevi[3]."

तस्मिन्नद्रौ कतिचिदबलाविप्रयुक्तः स कामी
    नीत्वा मासान्कनकवलयभ्रंशरिक्तप्रकोष्ठः ।
आषाढस्य प्रथमदिवसे मेघमाश्लिष्टसानुं

---

[1] Yakśās as per mythology are the attendants of Kubera, the Lord of wealth. They are demigods and hence deemed worthy of reverence. The name of this Yakśa has not been given in this lyric anywhere. This could be due to the norm that in holy texts names of those who flout the orders of their masters should not be mentioned. It is noteworthy in this lyric Mahākavi Kālidās has directly introduced the subject while in his other works he usually begins with a salutation to God or a benediction.

[2] Rāmgiri connotes the "mountain of Lord Rāma". The mountain is so named because Lord Rāma reputedly lived there for some time along with Laxman and Sitāji during their exile. It is identified by some with Chitrakuta in Bundelkhand.

[3] Dev. Sitā is believed to have taken a bath in the waters of Rāmgiri sanctifying them.

वप्रक्रीडापरिणतगजप्रेक्षणीयं ददर्श ।। २ ।।

Verse No. 2:

"This passionate (Yakśa),
Having a spent a few months,
On that mountain (of Rāmgiri),
Separated from (his) 'hapless beloved'[4],
(His) forearm being bereft,
Of the (usually worn) golden bracelet,
Having slipped from it;[5]
On the first day of Āṣādha,
(The Yakśa) beheld a Cloud,
Clinging to the mountain top,
(Which was) spectacular (like) an elephant,
Engaged in the game of butting the mountain,
With its tusks"

तस्य स्थित्वा कथमपि पुरः कौतुगाधानहेतो–
रन्तर्बाष्पश्चिरमनुचरो राजराजस्य दध्यौ ।
मेघालोके भवति सुखिनोऽप्यन्यथावृत्ति चेतः
कण्ठाश्लेषप्रणयिनि जने किं पुनर्दूरसंस्थे ।। ३ ।।

Verse No. 3:

"(This) follower of Kubera,
(His) tears (staunched) within,
Somehow stood for long ruminating,
In front of that (Cloud),
Being the cause of evoking (within him),
A fervent hope,
(Of sending a message to his beloved);

---

[4] The word used is "Abala". While this means a woman generally, here the Mahākavi wishes to stress the suffering aspect of Yakśa's wife in the absence of her Lord.

[5] This is how Kālidās typically describes a lover growing emaciated due to the anguish of separation from his beloved. King Duşyant is similarly depicted when he was suffering from remorse due to his repudiation of Śakunatalā without there being any fault on her side.

Even the mood of a happy lover,
Becomes otherwise,
After having sighted a cloud [6];
What to speak of,
When such a lover,
Seeking to embrace the neck (of his beloved),
Happens to be far away (from her)"

प्रत्यासन्ने नभसि दयिताजीवितालम्बनार्थी
जीमूतेन स्वकुशलमयीं हारयिष्यन्प्रवृत्तिम।
स प्रत्यग्रैः कुटजकुसुमैः कल्पितार्घाय तस्मै
प्रीतः प्रीतिप्रमुखवचनं स्वागतं व्याजहार ।। ४ ।।

Verse No. 4:

"With approaching of the month of Śrāvana,
Seeking to sustain the life of (his) beloved[7],
(Desirous) (hence) of conveying the tidings,
Of his well-being through the Cloud,
He (the Yakśa) having ritualistically offered[8],
Freshly bloomed 'Kutajā' flowers to it (the Cloud),
Being in a happy frame of mind,[9]
Bid him welcome,
Saying mostly loving words"

---

[6] The Mahākavi here is implying that by merely observing a cloud strong romantic impulses surge in people, and they get somewhat jittery even if they are with their loved ones.

[7] In the month of Śrāvana, being the rainy season, there is an upsurge in romantic longings. Lovers who are away from their partners then become highly agitated. This is why the Yakśa had become overly anxious about the well-being of his wife who was far away, especially with the approaching of Śrāvana.

[8] Life is sustained by water of which Clouds are the source. This is why the Yakśa deemed the Cloud worthy of worship. Moreover, the Cloud was his honoured guest from whom he intended to seek the favour of taking a message to his beloved wife.

[9] Since at long last, the Yakśa had found a way of sending a message to his wife, he was in a happy frame of mind.

धूमज्योतिःसलिलमरुतां संनिपातः क्व मेघः
    संदेशार्थाः क्व पटुकरणैः प्राणिभिः प्रापणीयाः।
इत्यौत्सुक्यादपरिगणयन्गुह्यकस्तं ययाचे
    कामार्ता हि प्रकृतिकृपणाश्चेतनाचेतनेषु ॥ ५ ॥

Verse No. 5:

"Where (this) Cloud,
A (mere) conglomeration,
Of smoke, fire, water (and) wind,
(And) where the beings,
Conveyers of contents of messages,
(Possessed) of organs suited for this purpose[10];
(But) out of (excessive) zeal,
(To send the message),
"Not taking all this into account,
The Yakśa entreated him (the Cloud);
Those who are tormented by passionate longings,
Verily becoming confused temperamentally,
As regards sentience and the insentience"

जातं वंशे भुवनविदिते पुष्करावर्तकानां
    जानामि त्वां प्रकृतिपुरुषं कामरूपं मघोनः।
तेनार्थित्वं त्वयि विधिवशाद्दूरबन्धुर्गतोऽहं
    याच्ञा मोघा वरमधिगुणे नाधमे लब्धकामा ॥ ६ ॥

Verse No. 6:

"Born in the world-renowned clan,
Of Puṣkarās and Avartakās,
I know you as the principal agent of Indra[11],
Capable of assuming any form,
As per (your) volition[12];

---

[10] Faculty of intelligence is presupposed for a messenger. It is lacking in an inanimate being like the Cloud. This is why Mahākavi Kālidās attracted much fame in those times by his choice of the "Cloud" to play the central role of a messenger in this seminal lyric.

[11] Indra is the Lord of firmaments, the purveyor of rains. Hence the Cloud is depicted as his principal agent in this verse.

Myself being far away from a dear one (my wife),
As decreed by fate;
Hence to you am I petitioning;
Preferable an entreaty to a virtuous person,
(Even if) to prove futile,
Than the one made to a knave,
(Even if) proving fruitful"

संतप्तानां त्वमसि शरणं तत्पयोद ! प्रियाया:
संदेशं मे हर धनपतिक्रोधविश्लेषितस्य ।
गन्तव्या ते वसतिरलका नाम यक्षेश्वराणां
बाह्योद्यानस्थितहरशिरश्चन्द्रिकाधौतहर्म्या ।। ७ ।।

Verse No. 7:

"Oh Cloud ! you are the refuge of the distressed[13],
So bear my message,
To my beloved,
Separated as I am (from her),
By the wrath of the Lord of Wealth,
(The Kubera);
The abode of the Lords of Yakśās (Kubera)[14],
Named as Alakā,[15]
Being your destination;
Its mansions being illumined by rays of the moon,
Ensconced on the head of Śivaji,
Residing in the garden outside (Alakā)"

त्वामारूढं पवनपदवीमुद्गृहीतालकान्ता:
प्रेक्षिष्यन्ते पथिकवनिता: प्रत्ययादाश्वसत्य: ।

---

[12] Elsewhere too clouds have been portrayed as capable of taking up any shape. Quoting from Socrates -- "Clouds can assume what shapes they will, believe me" [From the Meghadūtam by Mahakavi Kālidās; translated by M. R. Kāle, Page 17]

[13] The Cloud is so depicted as it gives relief to those suffering from the heat of summer.

[14] The plural term 'Lords' is used in an honorific way for Kubera.

[15] This is the capital of Kubera renowned for its unimaginable wealth.

क: संनद्धे विरहविधुरां त्वय्युपेक्षेत जायां
न स्यादन्योऽप्यहमिव जनो य: पराधीनवृत्ति: ।। ८ ।।

Verse No. 8:

"(While) perched you are,
On the path of wind,
Wives of those away travelling,
Will look at you,
Pushing back extremities of (their) tresses,
(Away from their faces)[16],
Reassured by the confidence;
(In the safe return of their husbands)[17];
With you (thus) spread across (in the sky),
Who can be unmindful of (his) wife[18],
(That one) being tormented by separation,
(From her loved one);
Provided he is someone,
Not like me too,
Dependent on others"

तां चावश्यं दिवसगणनातत्परामेकपत्नी-
मव्यापन्नामविहतगतिर्द्रक्ष्यसि भ्रातृजायाम् ।
आशाबन्ध: कुसुमसदृशं प्रायशो ह्यङ्गनानां
सद्य:पाति प्रणयिहृदयं विप्रयोगे रुणद्धि ।। ९ ।।

Verse No. 9:

"(Oh! Cloud),

---

[16] It was believed that wives whose husbands were away for long became unmindful of their appearance. This is why in this verse women are portrayed as having dishevelled hair as their husbands were travelling. Hence their faces would be covered with hair. These women would push them back so as to get a better view of the Cloud.

[17] This is because the women had seen the Cloud which was deemed a favourable omen.

[18] The Cloud makes the beholder more romantically inclined and hence more anxious about his beloved, especially the one who is away. This applies to those travelling and hence separated from their dear ones.

(Moving) with steady gait,
You would undoubtedly behold,
The wife of (your) brother,
(The Yakśā's wife),
That one who is chaste (and) (somehow) surviving[19],
Wholly and solely engaged,
In counting the days,
(For the return of the Yakśa);
Verily the loving heart of women,
Suddenly collapsible like a flower,
Is mostly held together,
During the (anguish) of separation,
By the bond of hope,
(As are the petals by its base)"

मन्दं मन्दं नुदति पवनश्चानुकूलो यथा त्वां
वामश्चायं नदति मधुरं चातकस्ते सगन्धः।
गर्भाधानक्षणपरिचयान्नूनमाबद्धमालाः
सेविष्यन्ते नयनसुभगं खे भवन्तं बलाकाः॥ १० ॥

Verse No. 10:

"Favourable breeze will propel you[20],
Gently and gently as desirable;
And to your left being,
This Chataka (bird),
A kith and kin of yours[21],
Cooing sweetly;
Arrayed in rows in the sky,
Having experienced the joy of conception[22],

---

[19] It is implied that Yakśā's wife had only somehow remained clinging to her life being tormented by the anguish of separation from him.

[20] The Yakśa is explaining to the Cloud how various omens are auspicious for latter's journey such as favourable breeze, the presence of a Chataka bird to the left, etc; these are deemed to be propitious portents.

[21] As per folklore the Chataka bird sustains itself only by raindrops falling from the clouds. This is why the Mahākavi describes the Chataka bird as Cloud's kith and kin.

[22] As per folklore, it is the clouds which impregnate female cranes in the sky.

Are indeed female cranes,
Attending to you,
Yourself being (so) delightful to look at"

कर्तुं यच्च प्रभवति महीमुच्छिलीन्ध्रामबन्ध्यां
तच्छ्रुत्वा ते श्रवणसुभगं गर्जितं मानसोत्का:।
आकैलाशाद् बिसकिसलयच्छेदपाथेयवन्त:
सम्पत्स्यन्ते नभसि भवतो राजहंसा: सहाया: ।। ११ ।।

Verse No. 11:

"And having heard that melodious thunder of yours,
Which has the capability,
To make the earth,
Fertile (and) full of mushrooms[23],
The royal swans,
Eager to go to the Mānasa (Sarovar),
Carrying with them for sustenance,
During the journey,
Clumps of lotus stalks,
Will in the sky,
Turn into your companions,
Until the Kailaśa (mountain)[24]"

आपृच्छस्व प्रियसखममुं तुङ्गमालिङ्ग्य शैलं,
वन्द्यै: पुंसां रघुपतिपदैरङ्कितं मेखलासु ।
काले काले भवति भवतो यस्य संयोगमेत्य,
स्नेहव्यक्तिश्चिरविरहजं मुञ्चतो बाष्पमुष्णम् ।। १२ ।।

Verse No. 12:

---

[23] It is evident that Mahākavi Kālidās clearly appreciated that the entire earth constituted one unified ecosystem. He thus anticipated the modern environmentalists by many centuries.

[24] As per mythology, Kailāś is a mythical mountain made up of glittering gems which is the abode of Kubera as well as the favourite haunt of Śiva. It is north of the Mānasarovar. This is now a major centre of pilgrimage, though it is in Chinese territory. In subsequent verses we will come across many descriptions of the unimaginable wealth and magnificence of Kailās mountain.

"Having embraced this dear friend (of yours)[25],
The towering mountain (Ramagiri),
Its middle region being imprinted,
With the feet of Lord Rāma,
(Object of) veneration of people;
Seek its concurrence,
(And) bid it farewell;
(The mountain) from time to time,
Having received your companionship,
Whose affection (for you),
Is demonstrated,
By exhalation of warm sighs,[26]
Arising from long separation (from you)"[27]

मार्गं तावच्छृणु कथयतस्त्वत्प्रयाणानुरूपम्
संदेशं मे तदनु जलद श्रोष्यसि श्रोत्रपेयम् ।
खिन्नः खिन्नः शिखरिषु पदं न्यस्य गन्तासि यत्र
क्षीणः क्षीणः परिलघु पयः स्रोतसां चोपभुज्य ।। १३ ।।

Verse No. 13:

"Now (please) listen to the route,
Being narrated (by me),
Appropriate for your journey,
O Cloud, you will then hear,
My message (for my beloved),
(So) pleasant to the ear;
As you proceed from here,
Becoming weaker and weaker[28],

---

[25] In Sanskrit literature the ocean and the moon, the sun and the sun-lotus, etc., are depicted as natural friends; and so are the mountain and the cloud. This is because the latter by its showers cools the former. Embrace "your friend", the "mountain", is a metaphorical expression for 'let your waters come down upon it'.

[26] Figurative way of expressing hot steam emerging from baked earth after showers. This is beautiful imagery indeed.

[27] This is an allusion to the Cloud commencing its annual journey in the monsoon season from the Ramagiri mountain.

Rest (your) foot an mountain-tops;
And drink the easily digestible (and) light water of streams,
As you turn thinner and thinner[29]"

अद्रेः श्रृङ्गं हरति पवनः किंस्विदित्युन्मुखीभिः,
दृष्टोत्साहश्चकितचकितं मुग्धसिद्धाङ्गनाभिः।
स्थानादस्मात्सरसनिचुलादुत्पतोदङ्मुखः खं,
दिङ्नागानां पथि परिहरन् स्थूलहस्तावलेपान् ।। १४ ।।

Verse No. 14:

"From this place of wet 'Nichula'[30],
Soar into the firmaments,
In the northern direction;
The vigour (of your thrusts and movements),
Being gazed at with great amazement,
With upturned faces,
By the simple-minded wives,
Of the Siddhas[31];
(Wondering) if possibly,
The wind is spiriting away,
The peak of the mountain;
(But) (Oh ! Cloud) on the way,
Keeping (well) away,
From the slashings of huge trunks,
Of the quarter-elephants"[32]

रत्नच्छायाव्यतिकर इव प्रेक्ष्यमेतत् पुरस्तात्
वल्मीकाग्रात् प्रभवति धनुःखण्डमाखण्डलस्य ।

---

[28] The Cloud is heavy as it is full of water. Hence it is portrayed as becoming weak due to movement.

[29] As the Cloud loses water, it is figuratively depicted as growing thin.

[30] Nichula is a kind of cane growing on wetlands as found on mountain tops. The Yakśa is describing the Cloud's take-off location.

[31] The Siddhas are deemed to be semi-divine beings who are inhabitants of the Kailaś mountain.

[32] As per mythology, each of the eight directions has a guardian pair of elephants (male and female) assigned to it.

येन श्यामं वपुरतितरां कान्तिमापत्स्यते ते
बर्हेणेव स्फुरितरुचिना गोपवेषस्य विष्णोः ।। १५ ।।

Verse No. 15:

"(Here on the Rāmgiri mountain),
Over an ant-hill ahead of (me, Yakśa),[33]
Is emerging a spectacular fragment of a rainbow,
Resembling mixing of hues,
Of various gems;
By which will acquire,
Your dark body,
Exceeding charm;
Just as is (imparted) by the scintillating radiance[34],
Of the peacock feather,
(To the dark complexion)
Of Lord Vishnu attired as a cowherd"

त्वय्यायत्तं कृषिफलमिति भ्रूविलासानभिज्ञैः
प्रीतिस्निग्धैर्जनपदवधूलोचनैः पीयमानः ।
सद्यः सीरोत्कषणसुरभि क्षेत्रमारुह्य मालं
किञ्चित् पश्चात् व्रज लघुगतिर्भूय एवोत्तरेण ।। १६ ।।

Verse No. 16:

"In view of the dependence,
On you of agricultural produce,
You will be admiringly gazed at,
By (simple-minded) village ladies,
With eyes moist out of affection,
(Though) not acquainted,
With the coquettish movement of eyebrows;
Mover over (then) the (mountainous) plateau,
(Called) Malam;

---

[33] This stanza as the earlier one describes the scenario where the Yakśa is situated.

[34] The Yakśa is thus encouraging the Cloud to move on for carrying out the mission of giving a message to his beloved. This is by suggesting that the Cloud would come to possess a dazzling appearance on the way.

(And) (make them) fragrant,[35]
Having been just ploughed,
(By drenching them with your waters);
Move a little westwards,
(And) then again at a rapid gait[36],
Northwards only"

त्वामासारप्रशमितवनोपप्लवं साधु मूर्ध्ना
वक्ष्यत्यध्वश्रमपरिगतं सानुमानाम्रकूटः ।
न क्षुद्रोऽपि प्रथमसुकृतापेक्षया संश्रयाय,
प्राप्ते मित्रे भवति विमुखः किं पुनर्यस्तथोच्चैः ।। १७ ।।

Verse No. 17:
"Having extinguished the blaze,
In (its) (mountain's) wooden regions,
By (your) showers (earlier),
The Amrakut mountain,[37]
Will bear gingerly by (its) head (the peak),
Yourself, thoroughly exhausted by the journey,
With every decorum;
Even a lowly person,
Doesn't disregard,
A friend who has turned up,
For shelter,
Keeping in view,
His earlier benevolent action;
What to speak then,
Of somebody exalted,
Like the (mountain)"

छन्नोपान्तः परिणतफलद्योतिभिः काननाम्रै–

[35] It is well known that when the hot earth receives the first rains of the summer a pleasant emanation arises from it making the ground fragrant.
[36] The Cloud is lighter having emptied its belly of water. This is why as per the Mahākavi his gait becomes lighter and quicker.
[37] The Amrakut mountain is situated as per some commentators east of the Vindhya range and is the fountainhead of various rivers like the Narmadā.

स्त्वय्यारूढे शिखरमचल: स्निग्धवेणीसवर्णे ।
नूनं यास्यत्यमरमिथुनप्रेक्षणीयामवस्थां
मध्ये श्याम: स्तन इव भुव: शेषविस्तारपाण्डु: ।। १८ ।।

Verse No. 18:

"With forests of mango trees,
Gorgeous due to (their) ripe fruit,
Covering the grounds,
Of the (Amrakut) mountain;
When yourself (Oh ! Cloud),
Be on its top,
Having the colour of soft, smooth braid of hair;
Will it indeed (then) assume,
(Splendid) appearance like that of earth's breast,
Darkish in the middle[38],
(And) pale yellowish elsewhere[39],
Worthy of being gazed at,
By celestial couples"

स्थित्वा तस्मिन् वनचरवधूभुक्तकुञ्जे मुहूर्तं,
तोयोत्सर्गंद्रुततरगतिस्तत्परं वर्त्म तीर्ण: ।
रेवां द्रक्ष्यस्युपलविषमे विन्ध्यपादे विशीर्णां
भक्तिच्छेदैरिव विरचितां भूतिमङ्गे गजस्य ।। १९ ।।

Verse No. 19:

"Having stayed for a while,
On it (The Amrakut mountain),
In whose arbour,
Wives of foresters recreate themselves;
(After) discharging the waters (of your belly),
Traverse at a faster gait,
The onward path;

---

[38] The simile of earth's breast is applied to the mountain in the middle of which is the dark 'Cloud'. The latter by implication is like a nipple. Areas around the peak are whitish due to profusion of mango trees laden with ripe mangos.
[39] --ibid--

You would observe,
In the valley of Vindhya (mountain),
With stones and boulders of uneven size,
(Strewn across),
The (river) Rewā[40] (spread) all over,
Seemingly like a design on elephant's body[41],
Patterned by ornamental lines"

तस्यास्तिक्तैर्वनगजमदैर्वासितं वान्तवृष्टि-
जम्बूकुञ्जप्रतिहतरयं तोयमादाय गच्छेः ।
अन्तःसारं घन ! तुलयितुं नानिलः शक्ष्यति त्वां
रिक्तः सर्वो भवति हि लघुः पूर्णता गौरवाय ।। २० ।।

Verse No. 20:

"(After) sending down (your) showers,
Proceed, taking her (Nārmadā's) waters,
Scented by the ichor,
Fragrant yet astringent,
Of wild elephants;
(And) its currents,
Obstructed by clumps,
Of 'Jāmun' trees;
Oh ! Cloud,
Having been invested,
With (stupendous) strength within[42],
The wind won't be able,
To buffet you here and there;
All (those) hollow within,
Verily become insignificant,
(While) perfection leads to honour[43]"

---

[40] The 'Reva' river is the Narmadā river of our era.

[41] This is a beautiful and apt imagery. Both the elephant's skin and the earth being dark and grey, they provide a similar background, be it the design on elephant's back or the white waters of Narmadā crisscrossing the valley.

[42] When the Cloud becomes filled with water.

[43] This brings out the uncanny ability of the Mahakavi to weave together precepts of ethics with happenings of daily life. This shows that the Mahakavi

नीपं दृष्ट्वा हरितकपिशं केसरैरर्धरूढै
राविर्भूतप्रथममुकुलाः कन्दलीश्चानुकच्छम् ।
जग्ध्वारण्येष्वधिकसुरभिं गन्धमाघ्राय चोर्व्याः
सारङ्गास्ते जललवमुचः सूचयिष्यन्ति मार्गम् ।। २१ ।।

Verse No. 21:

"(While going onwards),
The bees, deer and elephants,[44]
Will indicate the (correct) path,
To you emitting water drops;
The bees having looked at,
(Multi-hued) Kadamba flowers,
Green, dark and red or yellow,
Due to half - grown filaments;
And the deer having consumed,
The Kandalī plants around the marshy land,
Buds thereof making an appearance,
For the first time;[45]
And elephants having smelt the earth's odour,
So very fragrant,
In the forests"[46]

अम्भोबिन्दुग्रहणचतुरांश्चातकान् वीक्षमाणाः
श्रेणीभूताः परिगणनया निर्दिशन्तो बलाकाः ।
त्वामासाद्य स्तनितसमये मानयिष्यन्ति सिद्धाः
सोत्कम्पानि प्रियसहचरीसम्भ्रमालिङ्गितानि ।। २२ ।।

Verse No. 22:

---

attached greatest importance to a person possessing strength and moral character.

[44] The bees, deer and elephants get exhilarated in the monsoon. This is why the Mahakavi has portrayed them as "guides" for the Cloud.

[45] Only in the monsoon the Kadamba flowers bloom and the 'Kandalī' plant bears flowers.

[46] This testifies to the rich flora and fauna in those days - a testimony to the pure, pollution-free environment of that era.

"The Siddhās,
Counting the female cranes,
Arrayed in rows,
By pointing at (them);
The Siddhas (also) gazing admiringly,
At the Chataka birds[47],
Dexterous in picking up drops of rain water;
They will highly regard you,
Having received embraces,
(Given) agitatedly,
In bewilderment,
By (their) beloved companions[48],
Upon (your) (sudden) thunder"

उत्पश्यामि द्रुतमपि सखे मत्प्रियार्थं यियासोः,
कालक्षेपं ककुभसुरभौ पर्वते पर्वते ते ।
शुक्लापाङ्गैः सजलनयनैः स्वागतीकृत्य केकाः
प्रत्युद्यातः कथमपि भवान् गन्तुमाशु व्यवस्येत् ।। २३ ।।

Verse No. 23:
"My friend (Oh ! Cloud),
Though wishing to proceed fast,
To do something dear to me,
I envisage your tarrying,
From one mountain to another,[49]
Fragrant with 'Kutaja' (flowers);
By peacocks, tearful of eyes,[50]
Having rendered (their) cooing;[51]

---

[47] This is a mythical bird repeatedly referred to in Sanskrit literature. It drinks falling rain drops in the sky only (and not after they have reached the ground).
[48] Shows Mahakavi's intimate knowledge of female psychology and man's natural protective instinct.
[49] We all know that mountains receive maximum rains. The Mahakavi has expressed this notion in a highly poetic manner by saying that the 'Cloud' will be delayed from one mountain top to another.
[50] The peacocks become exuberant in the rainy season and dance with abandon. This is why their eyes become full of tears of joy at the sight of the Cloud.
[51] An excellent imagery.

Welcoming you;
(After) having received (such) hospitality,
Somehow or other,
May your honour attempt,
To move on quickly"

पाण्डुच्छायोपवनवृतयः केतकैः सूचिभिन्नै
नीडारम्भैर्गृहबलिभुजामाकुलग्रामचैत्याः ।
त्वय्यासन्ने परिणतफलश्यामजम्बूवनान्ताः,
सम्पत्स्यन्ते कतिपयदिनस्थायिहंसाः दशार्णाः ।। २४ ।।

Verse No. 24:

"With you being (soon),
In the proximity of Daśārṇa[52] (region),
Its hedges being its gardens,
Of whitish-yellow hue,
Thanks to (profusion) of "Ketaki" flowers,
Just blooming (opening up) at the top;
Noisy being its village temples,
With the nest-building (activities),
Of local birds;[53]
Charming would be the dark Jāmbu forests,
Due to ripened fruits,
(And which) would be the habitation,
Of royal swans,
For a few days"[54]

तेषां दिक्षु प्रथितविदिशालक्षणां राजधानीं,
गत्वा सद्यः फलमविकलं कामुकत्वस्य लब्धा ।
तीरोपान्तस्तनितसुभगं पास्यसि स्वादु यस्मात्,
सभ्रूभङ्गं मुखमिव पयो वेत्रवत्याश्चलोर्मि ।। २५ ।।

---

[52] It is believed that Daśārṇa region corresponds to present day Bundelkhand.
[53] By local birds are meant birds like crows.
[54] The presence of swans would lead to further enhancing the beauty of this region encircled by spectacular gardens of just blooming Ketaki flowers.

Verse No. 25:

"No sooner is reached,
Vidiśā, famed all over,
The capital city of theirs (Daśārṇas);
The perfect reward of (your) licentiousness,[55]
Would then be gained (by you);
Since you would drink,
The sweet and rippled water,
Of river Vetravati[56],
In a charming manner,
Having thundered close to her shores;
(Like a lover),
(Sucking gently the) the lower lip (of his beloved),
Her eyebrows knitted."[57]

नीचैराख्यं गिरिमधिवसेस्तत्र विश्रामहेतो
स्त्वत्सम्पर्कात् पुलकितमिव प्रौढपुष्पैः कदम्बैः ।
यः पण्यस्त्रीरतिपरिमलोद्गारिभिर्नागराणा-
मुद्दामानि प्रथयति शिलावेश्मभिर्यौवनानि ।। २६ ।।

Verse No. 26:

"There is (nearby) a mountain called 'Nichaih' [58]
Stay there for rest;
Due to close proximity with you,
(That mountain),
Will seemingly (betray) horripilation,
Through blooming Kadamba flowers[59];

---

[55] Throughout the Meghadūta the Mahākavi has portrayed in romantic terms the mutually complementary relationship (involving give and take of water) between the 'Cloud' and various rivers. He thus brings out the symbiotic unity of the ecosystem which has been acknowledged and highlighted by modern science only in present times.

[56] The river 'Vetravati' is river 'Betwah' of modern era. It flows into river Yamunā after traversing northwards of the Vindhya mountain chain.

[57] The knitted eyebrows correspond to water ripples.

[58] Mountain Nichais is close to the Vidiśā city (verse 25) which the Cloud has now left behind.

It (the mountain) manifests,
The unbridled youthful vigour,
Of inhabitants of the city,
By the fragrance,
Emitted by (its) rock caves,
(Produced) during lovemaking,
Of the women of easy virtue"

विश्रान्त: सन् व्रज वननदीतीरजातानि सिञ्च-
न्नुद्यानानां नवजलकणैर्यूथिकाजालकानि ।
गण्डस्वेदापनयनरुजाक्लान्तकर्णोत्पलानाम्,
छायादानात् क्षणपरिचित: पुष्पलावीमुखानाम् ।। २७ ।।

Verse No. 27:
"Proceed having rested,
(On that mountain)[60],
Sprinkling by fresh water drops,
The buds of Jasmine (flowers),
Having come up,
In the gardens (there),
On the banks of the rivulets of the forest;
Momentarily presenting yourself,
By imparting a sheen[61],
To the faces of (ladies),
Plucking flowers,
Lotuses in (their) ears faded,
By the strain of wiping off,
Sweat from (their) cheeks"

---

[59] These correspond to erect hair. This is why the Mahākavi has described Kadamba flowers as fully grown or blooming which makes it easy to identify them with hair bristling at the time of horripilation.

[60] This is mountain 'Nichaih' alluded to in the previous verse (No. 26)

[61] We all know that when a cloud passes overhead it casts a shadow momentarily on those below. It gives a distinctive 'sheen' to their faces. This has been portrayed elegantly by the Mahākavi as "presenting yourself (or making your "parichay"). No wonder it is Kālidās and Kālidās alone who is known by the moniker "Mahakavi" (Great Poet).

वक्र: पन्था: यदपि भवत: प्रस्थितस्योत्तराशां
सौधोत्सङ्गप्रणयविमुखो मास्म भूरुज्जयिन्या: ।
विद्युद्दामस्फुरितचकितैस्तत्र पौराङ्गनानाम्,
लोलापाङ्गैर्यदि न रमसे लोचनैर्वञ्चितोऽसि ।। २८ ।।

Verse No. 28:

"Proceeding northwards,[62]
Even if circuitous has to be your path,
Do not remain unfamiliar with the upper reaches,
Of the palaces of Ujjaini[63] [64];
If you are not enchanted,
By the eyes of the city ladies there,
With (their) tremulous glances (betraying) amazement,[65]
At the flashes,
Of streaks of (your) lightening,
(Surely) in vain has been,
(Your life)."

वीचिक्षोभस्तनितविहगश्रेणिकाञ्चीगुणाया:
संसर्पन्त्या: स्खलितसुभगं दर्शितावर्तनाभे: ।
निर्विन्ध्याया: पथि भव रसाभ्यन्तर: सन्निपत्य
स्त्रीणामाद्यं प्रणयवचनं विभ्रमो हि प्रियेषु ।। २९ ।।

Verse No. 29:

"(Like a maiden),
The Nirvindhyā river stumbles gracefully,
(over the rocks),
While gliding (forward),
The flight of birds (overhead),

---

[62] The Cloud is proceeding northwards from Devagiri, now Devagadh, in central India, to the abode of Kubera across the Himālayās. The city of Ujjaini does not lie on the straight path and therefore he is asked to make a detour.

[63] Ujjaini is modern Ujjain. Throughout this translation the term 'Ujjaini' has been used as in the original text.

[64] There are repeated allusions to Ujjaini in this lyric presumably because of the close association of the Mahākavi with it.

[65] This indicates that the ladies in that era were relaxed and happy.

Noisy due to turbulence of its currents,
(Like) a (jingling) waistband (of a maiden),
The river manifesting the eddies,
[Like a maiden exposing] the naval; [66]
Verily, the first expression of love,[67]
Of ladies towards their lovers,
Is through an amorous gesture;
On the way to Nirvindhyā,
Having come into contact with her,
Be the one full of exhilaration,
Having (absorbed)(her) waters[68]"

वेणीभूतप्रतनुसलिलाऽसावतीतस्य सिन्धुः
पाण्डुच्छाया तटरुहतरुभ्रंशिभिर्जीर्णपर्णैः ।
सौभाग्यं ते सुभग विरहावस्थया व्यञ्जयन्ती
कार्श्यं येन त्यजति विधिना स त्वयैवोपपाद्यः ।। ३० ।।

Verse No. 30:

"That river (Nirvindhyā),
Reduced to a trickle of water,[69]
(Like) a single braid of hair,
Being sickly (yellowish) of complexion,[70]
Due to worn-out leaves falling into her,
From trees grown on (its) banks;
Oh! (Cloud), the fortunate one,
By (this) love-lorn condition of (hers),
The river proclaims the good fortune,

---

[66] The river thus is clearly inviting the Cloud.

[67] A romantic relationship is envisaged in Sanskrit poetry between clouds and rivers based on their interdependence. In this verse the Nirvindhyā river is depicted as the beloved of the 'Cloud'.

[68] The Cloud is urged to freely make advances towards the river in view of her overtures revealing herself. (see footnote 66). Evidently there was "Me too" movement even in those days as men dared not take liberties with women without their consent.

[69] The river (a metaphor for a lovelorn lady) is thinned out and has yellowish pallor in the absence of her lover, the 'Cloud'.

[70] -ibid-

Of yourself, the wanderer;[71]
By whatever process,
The river would relinquish,
The emaciated condition (of hers),
That verily should be effected,
By you"

प्राप्यावन्तीनुदयनकथाकोविदग्रामवृद्धान्
पूर्वोद्दिष्टामुपसर पुरीं श्रीविशालां विशालाम् ।
स्वल्पीभूते सुचरितफले स्वर्गिणां गां गतानां,
शेषैः पुण्यैर्हृतमिव दिवः कान्तिमत् खण्डमेकम् ।। ३१ ।।

Verse No. 31:
"Having reached the region of Avanti[72],
Its old village folks,
Being well conversant with the legend of Udayan[73];
Approach (then) the city of Ujjaini,
Replete with opulence and charm,
As pointed out earlier;[74]
Being like a radiant piece of heaven,
Carried off by the remainder of merit,
Of denizens of heaven,
Having come down to earth,
With dwindling of fruits of (their) meritorious deeds"

दीर्घीकुर्वन् पटु मदकलं कूजितं सारसानाम्
प्रत्यूषेषु स्फुटितकमलामोदमैत्रीकषायः ।
यत्र स्त्रीणां हरति सुरतग्लानिमङ्गानुकूलः,
शिप्रावातः प्रियतम इव प्रार्थनाचाटुकारः ।। ३२ ।।

---

[71] The 'Cloud' is described as fortunate because the river has remained faithful to him in his absence and has become emaciated pining for him.
[72] This area lies north of the Narmadā river.
[73] He was the king of Vatsa region and his capital was Kausambi which is close to Prayagraj.
[74] There is a reference to Ujjaini in verse no. 28. The Cloud was told that he would get enchanted with the tremulous eyes of the women there.

Verse No. 32:

"Where (in the city of Ujjaini),
In the early morning,
The breeze blowing off the river Śipra[75],
Prolonging the distinctive cooing of cranes,
Its sweetness (tempered) by (their) by intoxication;
Agreeable to body being the breeze,
Pleasantly smelling being in contact,
With the fragrance of blooming lotuses;
It carries away the languor of women,
Arising after love making,
As if it (the breeze off the river Śiprā) was like a lover,
Carrying out sycophantic talk
Seeking the favour of love[76]"

हारांस्तारांस्तरलगुटिकान् कोटिशः शङ्खशुक्तीः
शष्पश्यामान् मरकतमणीनुन्मयूखप्ररोहान् ।
दृष्ट्वा यस्यां विपणिरचितान् विद्रुमाणाश्च भङ्गान्
संलक्ष्यन्ते सलिलनिधयस्तोयमात्रावशेषाः ॥ ३३ ॥

Verse No. 33:

"Wherein (in Ujjayini) having observed,
Necklaces of pure pearls,
Precious gems centring them[77];
Couches and pearl shells;
Emerald stones of (greenish hue),
(Like) tender green grass,
Rays shooting up from them,
(As if) sprouts[78];

---

[75] The city of Ujjaini stands on the banks of river Siprā or (Śiprā). It is noteworthy that the name of this river has remained unchanged during the last two thousand years.

[76] This throws interesting light on the mode of love-making in those days. It is apparent that women were always treated with tenderness and their feelings fully taken into account, even during moments of intimacy.

[77] Ujjayini undoubtedly was a fabulously wealthy city around two millennia ago. The description of its opulence is indeed mind boggling. No wonder India was to attract wave after wave of invaders intent on pillage and loot

And pieces of coral[79];
(All) in huge numbers,
Arranged in its markets;
It would appear;
What remains in the ocean,
Is nothing but water[80]"

प्रद्योतस्य प्रियदुहितरं वत्सराजोऽत्र जह्रे,
हैमं तालद्रुमवनमभूदत्र तस्यैव राज्ञः ।
अत्रोद्भ्रान्तः किल नलगिरिः स्तम्भमुत्पाट्य दर्पा-
दित्यागन्तून् रमयति जनो यत्र बन्धूनभिज्ञः ॥ ३४ ॥

Verse No. 34:
"It is here (in Ujjayini),
That the Vatsa king[81],
Abducted the beloved daughter[82],
Of Pradyota[83];
Of that monarch only,
Was here a forest,
Of 'Tāl' trees wrought of gold;
Reputedly (only) here,
Had roamed with bellicosity,
The (ferocious) elephant 'Nalagiri'[84],
Having uprooted (his) tethering pole,
In frenzy;
Where the knowledgeable people (in Ujjayini),
Entertain (their) folks,

---

[78] --ibid--

[79] --ibid--

[80] The ocean is regarded as a reservoir of jewels. The Mahākavi is implying that all the wealth of the ocean had moved away to Ujjayini leaving behind nothing but water.

[81] The name of this Vatsa king was Udayan.

[82] She was known as Vātsavadattā.

[83] Pradyota is also known as 'Chandamahāsena'.

[84] 'Nalagiri' was an extremely powerful elephant like Indra's Airāvat. He was bestowed upon Pradyota as a boon by goddess Chandi after harsh penance by the former in the form of offering oblations of his own flesh. This is why Pradyota began to be called Chandamahāsena.

Coming from outside,
With such (folklore)"

पत्रश्यामा दिनकरहयस्पर्धिनो यत्र वाहाः
शैलोदग्रास्त्वमिव करिणो वृष्टिमन्तः प्रभेदात् ।
योधाग्रण्यः प्रतिदशमुखं संयुगे तस्थिवान्सः
प्रत्यादिष्टाभरणरुचयश्चन्द्रहासव्रणाङ्कैः ।। ३५ ।।

Verse No. 35:

"Where (in Ujjayini) are horses,
Greenish dark like leaves,
Rivalling the sun's steads;
Mountain (like) towering elephants,
Ichor streaming out,[85]
Showering rains,
Resembling yourself;
(Its) leading warriors having steadfastly faced,
Rāvana in battle[86];
Have abandoned (their) love of ornaments,
Thanks to the marks of scars,
Made by Rāvana's sword"

जालोद्गीर्णैरुपचितवपु: केशसंस्कारधूपै
र्बन्धुप्रीत्या भवनशिखिभिर्दत्तनृत्योपहार: ।
हर्म्येष्वस्या: कुसुमसुरभिष्वध्वखेदं नयेथा:,
लक्ष्मीं पश्यंल्ललितवनितापादरागाङ्कितेषु ।। ३६ ।।

Verse No. 36:

"(Oh! Cloud)
Becoming strong and nourished in body,

---

[85] This is how huge, powerful elephants of that era were customarily portrayed in the Sanskrit literature.

[86] Ujjayini is described as having been wrenched away from the heaven (see verse no. 31). Rāvana had once tried to carry off the Kailāś mountain to Lankā as he was a supreme devotee of Śivaji. (See verse 62) A battle had then ensued. This is how probably in the imagination of the Mahākavi warriors of Ujjayini which was a part of heaven and therefore of Kailāś confronted Rāvana in battle.

By the (emanations) of fragrant materials,
Streaming out of window lattices,
(Applied) to embellish the hair[87],
(Of the ladies of Ujjayini);
Being given the gift,
In the form of (display) of dancing,
By domesticated peacocks,
Of city residences,
Out of fraternal love;
Observing its (Ujjayini's) grandeur,
On the terraces of its palaces,
Suffused with the aroma of flowers,
(And) bearing the marks,
Of the (red) colouring dye,
(Applied) to the feet,
Of the beautiful ladies in them,
Remove (thus) the journey's fatigue"

भर्तुः कण्ठच्छविरिति गणैः सादरं वीक्ष्यमाणः
पुण्यं यायास्त्रिभुवनगुरोर्धाम चण्डीश्वरस्य ।
धूतोद्यानं कुवलयरजोगन्धिभिर्गन्धवत्या-
स्तोयक्रीडानिरतयुवतिस्नानतिक्तैर्मरुद्भिः ।। ३७ ।।

Verse No. 37:
"(Oh ! Cloud),
(Being) admiringly gazed at,
By the cohort (of Lord Śiva),
Endowed as you are,
With the complexion of (their) master's throat[88];
Proceed to the sacred abode of Chandiśwar[89],
The Master of three worlds;

---

[87] It is noteworthy that the ladies even in that ancient era of around two millennia ago went to great lengths to preserve and enhance the beauty of their hair, no less than what they do today.
[88] The Cloud with his dark blue hue resembles the throat of Śivaji.
[89] Chandiśwar is Śivaji, Chandi being another name for Pārvati. This shows idol worship was practised in India at least since the commencement of the Christian era.

(Therein) is a garden,
Swaying in the breeze,
(Blowing) off the (river) Gandhavatī[90];
Suffused with the aroma,
Of lotus pollens;
(As well as) scented by the materials,
(Applied) during bathing,
By damsels very much fond of,
Water sports[91]"

अप्यन्यस्मिन् जलधर महाकालमासाद्य काले
स्थातव्यं ते नयनविषयं यावदत्येति भानुः ।
कुर्वन्सन्ध्यावलिपटहतां शूलिनः श्लाघनीया-
मामन्द्राणां फलमविकलं लप्स्यसे गर्जितानाम् ।। ३८ ।।

Verse No. 38:
"Oh ! Cloud (Carrier of water),
Even if the (shrine) of Mahākala[92],
Was to be reached (by you),
During some period (other than evening),
Remain there,
Until the sun vanishes,
From your eyesight;
You will (then) gain,
The reward in entirety,
Of (your) staid thundering[93],
Having played the commendable role,

---

[90] There is indeed a small rivulet by this name flowing near Ujjayini. It is noteworthy that its name has remained unchanged over two millennia.

[91] The young girls in that era were indeed very uninhibited and no eyebrows were raised when they engaged in water sports applying sweet-smelling materials to their bodies. This tells a lot about the norms of public decency then prevailing.

[92] This is the same temple (of Chandiśwar) referred to in the previous stanza (no. 37). To this day it has remained one of the most sacred shrines in India, especially of Śivaji.

[93] The Mahākavi by the phrase 'staid thundering' probably wishes to convey rumbling of moderate intensity in a steady and not haphazard way.

Of producing the sounds of Pataha (a big drum),[94]
During the evening worship of Śivaji"

पादन्यासैः क्वणितरशनास्तत्र लीलावधूतै-
रत्नच्छायाखचितवलिभिश्चामरैः क्लान्तहस्ताः ।
वेश्यास्त्वत्तो नखपदसुखान् प्राप्य वर्षाग्रबिन्दू-
नामोक्ष्यन्ते त्वयि मधुकरश्रेणिदीर्घान् कटाक्षान् ।। ३९ ।।

Verse No. 39:

"The Devadasis[95] there (in the shrine of Mahākāla),
Will cast at you,
Long, (adoring) glances,
(Like) a row of bees;
Having received from you,
The first rain drops,
Soothing (their) nailmarks[96];
(They) wearied of hands,
By waving with abandon,
Chowries[97] having handles,
Scintillating with lustre of gems[98];
Waistbands jingling,
By stamping of foot"

पश्चादुच्चैर्भुजतरुवनं मण्डलेनाभिलीनः
सान्ध्यं तेजः प्रतिनवजपापुष्परक्तं दधानः ।
नृत्यारम्भे हर पशुपतेरार्द्रनागाजिनेच्छां
शान्तोद्वेगस्तिमितनयनं दृष्टभक्तिर्भवान्या ।। ४० ।।

---

[94] The evening worship of Śivaji is regarded as the most significant among the three Āaratis done during the day. A percussion instrument with distinctive notes called 'Nagādā' is played at this time even in present times. This percussion instrument was probably called 'Pataha' in Mahākavi's times. This brings out the continuity of ritualistic traditions in India.

[95] The Devadāsis in the era of the Mahākavi were evidently a happy and respected lot.

[96] Made during lovemaking.

[97] This betokens that the Devadāsis were accoutered almost in a regal way.

[98] --ibid--

Verse No. 40:

"(Oh ! Cloud),
Having then[99] encompassed in a circular shape,
The towering arms (of Śivaji),
(As if) a forest of (lofty) trees;
Assuming (thus) the radiance of the evening[100],
Red like fresh "Japa" flowers;
(Then) at the commencement,
Of (Śivaji's) (Tāndav) dance[101],
Spirit away (thus) his longing,
For the wet (with red blood) elephant hide[102],
(Yourself being of the same colour);
(Your) devotion,
Will be looked at by Pārvatī (Bhavanī)
With serene eyes,
(Her) agitation having abated[103]"

गच्छन्तीनां रमणवसतिं योषितां तत्र नक्तं
रुद्धालोके नरपतिपथे सूचिभेद्यैस्तमोभिः ।
सौदामन्या कनकनिकषस्निग्धया दर्शयोर्वी,
तोयोत्सर्गस्तनितमुखरो मास्म भूर्विक्लवास्ताः ।। ४१ ।।

Verse No. 41:

"There (in Ujjayini) in the (dead) of night,
Courting women,

---

[99] It may be noted that in the earlier stanza no. 38 the Cloud had reached the Mahākala temple in the evening. He continues to be there and therefore events in this stanza no. 40 are projected as taking place late in the evening. The word 'then' alludes here to the period subsequent to the evening Āarati.

[100] --ibid--

[101] Śivaji's Tāndav dance starts after the evening Āarati.

[102] Śivaji, as per mythology, subsequent to slaying a demon who had assumed the body of an elephant had performed the Tāndava dance having wrapped around himself its hide red with blood. Afterwards, he began to look upon it as an ornament and liked to wear it while engaged in Tāndava dance.

[103] Parvatiji would get agitated on observing the blood-stained hide around Śivaji. Thanks to the Cloud, the hide no longer being there, she would feel reassured.

Proceeding to the abode of (their) lovers,
Along the main thoroughfare,
With (their) vision blocked,
Due to (pitch) darkness,[104]
(So dense) as penetrable by a needle[105];
Show (them), (Oh ! Cloud), the lay of the land,
By the flash of (your) lightning;
(Like) the lustre of a streak of gold,
On a touchstone[106];
Do not be rumbustious,
(Either) in (your) outpourings of water,
(Or) thundering;
(Inwardly) agitated being they, [107]
(The damsels in love)"

तां कस्याश्चिद् भवनवलभौ सुप्तपारावतायां
नीत्वा रात्रिं चिरविलसिनात्खिन्नविद्युत्कलत्रः।
दृष्टे सूर्ये पुनरपि भवान्वाहयेदध्वशेषं
मन्दायन्ते न खलु सुहृदामभ्युपेतार्थकृत्याः ।। ४२ ।।

Verse No. 42:

"Due to prolonged flashing[108],
The lightning has turned languid[109];
Being the spouse[110],
(Of yourself, Oh ! Cloud);

---

[104] A figurative way of expressing dense darkness. That young ladies could go about freely in total darkness is a testimony to the excellent law-and-order situation then prevailing.

[105] The society was obviously very liberal and free mixing between sexes was in no way frowned upon.

[106] This is an apt simile. A bright streak of gold on the black touchstone corresponds to a bright flash of lightning against the dark sky.

[107] The internal turmoil of these young girls is easily understandable as they were proceeding for a secret rendezvous with their lovers.

[108] In Sanskrit literature the cloud is portrayed as a male partner while lightning as the female one. The first two lines of the verse are a metaphor describing how after a bout of intense love-making the female partner becomes exhausted.

[109] --ibid--

[110] --ibid--

(After) (yourself) having spent that night,[111]
On the terrace of some mansion,
Among roosting pigeons;
Your honour may (then) complete,
The rest of the journey,
As soon as the sun is observed once more;
Indeed those don't tarry,
Who have undertaken,
Fulfilment of (their) friends' mission"

तस्मिन् काले नयनसलिलं योषितां खण्डितानां
शान्तिं नेयं प्रणयिभिरतो वर्त्म भानोस्त्यजाशु ।
प्रालेयास्त्रं कमलवदनात् सोऽपि हर्तुं नलिन्याः
प्रत्यावृत्तस्त्वयि कररुधि स्यादनल्पाभ्यसूयः ।। ४३ ।।

Verse No. 43:

"Tears in the eyes of jilted damsels in love[112],
Have to be wiped off,
By (their) lovers at that time[113];
Move away quickly therefore,
From the sun's path,
(Who) too has returned,
To remove (their) tears (the dew)[114],
From the face (leaves) of (his beloved), the lotus[115], [116]
(With) yourself obstructing (sun's) rays,
He would become,
Extremely vengeful (towards you)" [117]

---

[111] In the previous stanza (no. 40) it was early night.

[112] It is implied that these ladies were waiting for their lovers who, however, had left them high and dry.

[113] The Cloud had spent the night on the terrace of some house in the company of roosting pigeons. (verse no. 42). At day break he resumed his journey. Therefore the phrase 'at that time' in this verse refers to a period shortly after sunrise.

[114] Dew drops which appear early in the morning are compared to tears.

[115] The lotus is commonly portrayed in Sanskrit literature as sun's beloved.

[116] The sun is trying to mollify his beloved, the lotus, by carrying away the dew drops (tears) from her face (leaves). This is a metaphor for a paramour wiping off the tears of his jilted lover.

गम्भीराया: पयसि सरितश्चेतसीव प्रसन्ने
छायात्माऽपि प्रकृतिसुभगो लप्स्यते ते प्रवेशम् ।
तस्मादस्या: कुमुदविशदान्यर्हसि त्वं न धैर्या-
न्मोघीकर्तुं चटुलशफरोद्वर्तनप्रेक्षितानि ।। ४४ ।।

Verse No. 44:

"Into the clear waters,
Of river Gambhīrā[118],
As if in (her) pure heart[119],
Will gain entry,
Your reflection too,
Being naturally pleasing;
Therefore out of (undue) forbearance,
You should not let go in vain,
Her (rolling and tremulous) glances,
Of lotus (like) purity,
(Like) the dartings of 'Śaphara' fish[120],
In (perpetual) movement"

तस्या: किंचित्करधृतमिव प्राप्तवानीरशाखं
हृत्वा नीलं सलिल-वसनं मुक्तरोधोनितम्बम् ।
प्रस्थानं ते कथमपि सखे! लम्बमानस्य भावि,
ज्ञातास्वादो विवृतजघनां को विहातुं समर्थ: ।।४५।।

Verse No. 45:

---

[117] This verse is truly a beautiful metaphor in which the lotus and the dew on it have been compared with the tears in the eyes of a jilted lover. The sun is the paramour.
All this is a figurative description of the commonly observed phenomenon of dew drying up in the early hours after sunrise. An excellent example of Mahakavi's flight of imagination.

[118] The Gambhīrā is a small river in central India.

[119] Gambhīrā's noble nature as a heroine is highlighted by commending the purity of her heart.

[120] The Śaphara fish with their rapid movements in and out of water is a simile for Gambhīrā's purported tremulous and rolling looks.

"Oh ! friend (Oh ! Cloud),
(Succumbing to Gambhīrā's bewitching looks)[121],
Having yanked off,
Her (covering of) blue water sheet[122],
Cane branches barely touching it,
As if weakly clutched by her hands[123];
(Thus) being exposed,
Her hip-banks;[124]
What now to say of your departure,
Yourself being supine (on her);
Having experienced the flavour (of union),
Who is capable of abandoning,
(One's lover), her thighs bare"

त्वन्निष्यन्दोच्छ्वसितवसुधागन्धसंपर्करम्य:
स्त्रोतोरन्ध्रध्वनितसुभगं दन्तिभि: पीयमान:।
नीचैर्वास्यत्युपजिगमिषोर्देवपूर्वं गिरिं ते
शीतोवायु: परिणमयिता काननोदुम्बराणाम् ।।४६।।

Verse No. 46:

"A cool breeze ripening "gular" fruits,
Of the forest;
Will blow below you, (Oh! Cloud),
Desirous of approaching,
The Devagiri[125] mountain;
The breeze being gulped up,

---

[121] In the preceding stanza no. 44 the Cloud is advised that he should not disregard Gambhīrā's coquettish looks. The Cloud is very much portrayed as a gentleman and on his own never makes advances. This also speaks about the high standards of chivalry then prevailing. Perhaps the 'Me too' movement is far older than we suspect.

[122] This is due to Gambhīrā's waters being absorbed by the Cloud.

[123] This is a figurative way of describing the branches of cane trees on the banks touching the receding blue waters of Gambhīrā. She is portrayed as a coy lover who with her hands (cane branches) is trying to hold on to her clothing.

[124] Receding water levels had exposed the banks of the Gambhīrā river. This is poetically put as her hips being uncovered.

[125] As per some scholars the Devagiri mountain is near a village called Devagad which is about 60 miles south-west of Jhānsi.

By elephants with a pleasant (gurgling) sound,
As it (passes) through the apertures,
Of (their) trunks;
Agreeable being the breeze,
By its intermingling,
With the fragrance of the earth,[126]
Puffed up,
Thanks to your showers"

तत्र स्कन्दं नियतवसतिं पुष्पमेघीकृतात्मा
पुष्पासारैः स्नपयतु भवान् व्योमगङ्गाजलार्द्रैः।
रक्षाहेतोर्नवशशिभृता वासवीनां चमूना-
मत्यादित्यं हुतवहमुखे संभृतं तद्धि तेजः ॥४७॥

Verse No. 47:

"(Oh ! Cloud),
(After reaching) there,
(The Devagiri mountain) [127],
Turning yourself into a flowery cloud,
Your Honor may bathe,
(Lord) Skanda, permanently residing on it [128],
By a shower of flowers,
Wetted by the waters,
Of the heavenly Ganges;
Verily (Skanda) being the incandescence,
More potent than of the sun,
That has been concentrated in the mouth of Agni,
(By Śivaji),[129]
Bearer of the lunar crescent (young moon);
(And that) with a view to protection,
The armies of Indra"

---

[126] It is a common experience that when the hot earth is cooled by first showers of monsoon, it puffs up a little and emits a pleasant aroma.

[127] The Cloud's journey northwards as chalked out by the Yakśa continues. In the preceding stanza (No.46), the Cloud is approaching the Devagiri mountain.

[128] After having slain a ferocious demon named Tarakāsur, the gods had granted Skanda the boon of permanent residence on the Devagiri mountain.

[129] Skanda was a mirror image of Śivaji in terms of his prowess, potency, etc.

ज्योतिर्लेखावलयि गलितं यस्य बर्हं भवानी
पुत्रप्रेम्णा कुवलयदलप्रापि कर्णे करोति ।
धौतापाङ्गं हरशशिरुचा पावकेस्तन्मयूरं
पश्चादद्रिग्रहणगुरुभिर्गर्जितैर्नर्तयेथा: ।।४८।।

Verse No. 48:

"Afterwards (having ritualistically bathed Skanda)[130],
Induce his peacock to dance,
By (your) thundering,
Magnified (after) being absorbed,
(And echoed) by the mountain[131];
That peacock the outer corners,
Of whose eyes are very radiant,
Due to the lustre,
Of the lunar crescent of Śivaji;
Whose dropped off feather,
Bearing bright, circular streaks,
Out of affection for (her) son[132]
Parvatiji puts in (her) ear,
(Appropriately) the seat of a lotus petal"

आराध्यैनं शरवणभवं देवमुल्लङ्घिताध्वा
सिद्धद्वन्द्वैर्जलकणभयाद्वीणिभिर्मुक्तमार्गः ।
व्यालम्बेथाः सुरभितनयालम्भजां मानयिष्यन्,
स्त्रोतोमूर्त्या–भुवि परिणतां रन्तिदेवस्य कीर्तिम् ।।४९।।

Verse No. 49:

"(Oh ! Cloud),
After worshipping this god (Skanda),
Born of clusters of Śarā[133],

---

[130] See verse no. 47.

[131] This refers to the Devagiri mountain, the place of permanent residence of Skanda or Kartikeya. See verse no. 47.

[132] Skanda is the son of Parvatiji and Śivaji.

[133] Śara is a kind of reed.

(And) having traversed some distance,
Unimpeded being (your) path,
With lute-carrying Siddha[134] pairs,
(Remaining away from it),
Apprehensive lest (your) water drops,
(Come down on their lutes);
Adopt (then) a supine posture,
For paying homage,
To the river (Charmnavatī)
Its form being the transmogrification,
On the earth,
Of the glory of Rantideva,[135]
Ensuing from (his) cow sacrifice[136]"

त्वय्यादातुं जलमवनते शार्ङ्गिणो वर्णचौरे
तस्याः सिन्धोः पृथुमपि तनुं दूरभावात् प्रवाहम् ।
प्रेक्षिष्यन्ते गगनगतयो नूनमावर्ज्य दृष्टीः
एकं मुक्तागुणमिव भुवः स्थूलमध्येन्द्रनीलम् ।।५०।।

Verse No. 50:
"With yourself (Oh ! Cloud) sharing the complexion[137],
Of Lord Viṣṇu,
(And) engaged in imbibing the waters,
Of that river (Charmṇavatī) [138],
In a supine position (over it);
The denizens of firmaments,
Will (then) definitely observe,
(Their) vision focused,
The current of that river,

---

[134] They are devotees of Śivaji.
[135] King Rantideva had undertaken large-scale cow sacrifice; this river had resulted from their blood.
[136] This is the only reference in Mahākavi's writings to cow sacrifice. We find mention of cow slaughter in the Vedas (1500-2000 B.C.). Over the centuries the cow became an object of veneration, and therefore probably we find only a passing reference to this theme in Mahākavi's texts.
[137] The Cloud with his bluish dark colour resembles Lord Kriśna.
[138] See verse no. 49 giving the origin of this river.

(Seemingly) a trickle, though wide,
Due to the huge distance;
As if it were,
Earth's one-stringed pearl necklace,[139]
With a gorgeous blue sapphire, [140]
As its centre"

तामुत्तीर्य व्रज परिचितभ्रूलताविभ्रमाणां
पक्ष्मोत्क्षेपादुपरि विलसत्कृष्णशारप्रभाणाम् ।
कुन्दक्षेपानुगमधुकरश्रीमुषामात्मबिम्बं
पात्रीकुर्वन् दशपुरवधूनेत्रकौतूहलानाम् ॥५१॥

Verse No. 51:

"Proceed, having crossed it (the river Charmṇvatī)[141],
(While overflying the city of Daśapur),
The eyes of pretty ladies thereof,
Being familiar with the coquettish movements,
Of (their) vine-like eyebrows,
Flashing up dark, red and white lustres,
With their eyelids upturned;
These eyes (having so to say),
Carried away the beauty,
Of bees chasing the swaying Kunda flowers;[142]
Making your appearance worthy,
Of the admiration (for you),
In (such) eyes"

ब्रह्मावर्तं जनपदमथच्छायया गाहमानः

---

[139] The white waters of the river evoke a pearl necklace while the Cloud with his blue tinge bears verisimilitude with a gorgeous blue sapphire.

[140] --ibid--.

[141] This is mentioned in verse no. 49.

[142] The Kunda flower is white. The Mahākavi has compared black bees chasing Kunda flowers with eyes of Daśapur ladies. In this simile the pupil of the eye stands for the bee, while the outer portion of the eye corresponds to the white Kunda flower. This verse is an excellent example of Mahākavi's delightful imagery; only he could have turned the Cloud into an object evoking the admiration of damsels.

क्षेत्रं क्षत्रप्रधनपिशुनं कौरवं तद्व्रजेथाः ।
राजन्यानां शितशरशतैर्यत्र गाण्डीवधन्वा
धारापातैस्त्वमिव कमलान्यभ्यवर्षन् मुखानि ।।५२।।

Verse No. 52:

"Subsequent to (leaving behind Daśapur)[143]
(And) entering through (your) shadow,
The province of Brahmāvarta,
Proceed to that memorable region,
Of the Kurus,[144]
A pointer to the warfare,
Between the Kśatriyas;
Where (Arjuna), the wielder of the Gāndīva bow,
Showered the faces,
Of the kings,
With (his) innumerable sharp arrows;
Like yourself (Oh ! Cloud),
Showering the lotuses,
With cascading rains"

हित्वा हालामभिमतरसां रेवतीलोचनाङ्कां
बन्धुप्रीत्या समरविमुखो लाङ्गली याः सिषेवे ।
कृत्वा तासामधिगममपां सौम्य सारस्वतीनाम्-
अन्तःशुद्धस्त्वमपि भविता वर्णमात्रेण कृष्णः ।।५३।।

Verse No. 53:

"Balarāma shunned the battlefield,
(Of Kurukśetra),
Out of fraternal affection;
(And) abjured the (drinking of) wine,
(Though) relishing its flavour,
(And) bearing the reflection of Rewati's eyes;[145]

---

[143] See verse no. 51 alluding to the ladies of Daśapur.

[144] This connotes Kurukśetra which is in Haryana. In an earlier stanza no. 45 the Cloud was in the Devagad village in Jhansi. In this verse above (no. 51) he is over Haryānā. Thus, his northwards itinerary is being traced by the Mahākavi.

(And whose penance on the banks of Sāraswatī,
Had cleansed him of sin),[146]
Having partaken its (waters);[147]
(Similarly) having reached the waters,
Of that Sāraswatī,
(And) drunk them,
Oh ! gentle one, (Oh ! Cloud)
You too would become,
Internally pure,[148]
Dark (only) in complexion"

तस्माद् गच्छेरनुकनखलं शैलराजावतीर्णां
जह्नोः कन्यां सगरतनयस्वर्गसोपानपङ्क्तिम् ।
गौरीवक्त्रभ्रुकुटिरचनां या विहस्येव फेनैः
शंभोः केशग्रहणमकरोदिन्दुलग्नोर्मिहस्ता ।।५४।।

Verse No. 54:

"From there (Kurukśetra) proceed, (Oh ! Cloud),
To the neighbourhood of Kankhal[149]
(Where) descends,
From the Lord of the mountains (the Himālayās),
(The Ganges), the daughter of Jahnu,[150]

---

[145] Rewati was Balarām's wife and drinking companion. Therefore he observed reflection of her eyes in his wine.

[146] Sāraswatī existed in Vedic times. It has now become extinct. Many believed it to be mythical. But its dry bed connecting the Ganges with the Yamunā was discovered by archeologists in the last week of September, 2019. It then flew through Kurukśetra. Balarām was required to do penance for a year on its banks to atone for killing a Brāhmin.

[147] --ibid--

[148] So that the Cloud too becomes purged of sin accruing from his adulterous conduct with the rivers on the way.

[149] This is a place of pilgrimage near Haridwār where the Ganges touches the plains. It may be noted that the Cloud earlier (stanza no.52) was over Kurukśetra which is close to Kankhal

[150] Jahnu, the sage, had drunk the waters of the Ganges in anger when they had swept away his sacrificial grounds in the course of her descent to the earth. He had then let them out through his ear. This had earned him the moniker ' Father of Gangāji.

(Who) had (acted),
As a step-ladder to the heaven,[151]
For the sons of Sagar;
With (her) wave-like arms,
Clinging to the lunar (crescent),
The (Ganges) had grasped,
Śivaji's hair;[152]
(And) who by (her) froth,[153]
Derides as it were,
Formation of knitted brows,
On Pārvatiji's face,
(In annoyance)[154]"

तस्याः पातुं सुरगज इव व्योम्नि पश्चार्धलम्बी
त्वं चेदच्छस्फटिकविशदं तर्कयेस्तिर्यगम्भः ।
संसर्पन्त्या सपदि भवतः स्रोतसिच्छाययाऽसौ
स्यादस्थानोपगतयमुनासङ्गमेवाऽभिरामा ।।५५।।

Verse No. 55:

"(Oh ! Cloud)
Were you to ponder,
Over drinking her (of Ganges) waters,
Pure like a stainless crystal;[155]
As if you were Airavata,[156]
(Your) posterior half upraised in space,
(Somewhat) curved of posture;
Immediately then,
(With yourself so engaged in drinking the waters),
Alluring (indeed) would appear that (river),

---

[151] The Ganges after being brought down from the heavens had redeemed the souls of Sagar's sons when their ashes were immersed in her waters. She had thus acted figuratively as a pathway to heaven for them.
[152] This refers to the Ganges being enmeshed in Śivaji's matted hair.
[153] White froth is considered a symbol of derision.
[154] Pārvati's jealousy of the Gangāji is legendary both being Śivaji's co-wives.
[155] This is a striking testimony to the absolute purity of the waters of the Ganges in those days.
[156] Airāvata is the elephant of Indra.

With your (dark) shadow,
Gliding in (her) stream,
As if the (Ganges),
Were in conjunction with the Yamunā,[157]
Somewhere other than
its proper place of confluence"[158]

आसीनानां सुरभितशिलं नाभिगन्धैर्मृगाणां
तस्या एव प्रभवमचलं प्राप्य गौरं तुषारैः ।
वक्ष्यस्यध्वश्रमविनयने तस्य शृङ्गे निषण्णः
शोभां शुभ्रत्रिनयनवृषोत्खातपङ्कोपमेयाम् ॥५६॥

Verse No. 56:
"(Oh ! Cloud)
Having reached (that) mountain (the Himālayās),
White due to snowflakes,
Verily the fountainhead of that (river, the Ganges);
The rocks (of that mountain),
Being sweet-smelling due to the scent,[159]
(Emanating) from the naval,
Of the squatting deer;
With (yourself) perched on its peak,
In order ebbs away the journey's strain;
You (Oh ! Cloud) would embody the charm,
Comparable to a heap of mud,
Messed up by the White Bull,
Of the three-eyed God (Śivaji)

तं चेद्वायौ सरति सरलस्कन्धसंघट्टजन्मा
बाधेतोल्काक्षपितचमरीबालभारो दवाग्निः ।
अर्हस्येनं शमयितुमलं वारिधारासहस्त्रै

[157] This is a particularly apt simile as the dark shadow of the Cloud in the white waters of the Ganges would indeed resemble dark waters of the Yamunā flowing into her.
[158] Place apart from Prayāg.
[159] This alludes to the fragrance of Kasturi (musk).

रापन्नार्तिप्रशमनफलाः सम्पदो ह्युत्तमानाम् ।।५७।।

Verse No. 57:

"In the blowing wind,
By the friction,
Between the branches of Sarala trees,
Having flared up a forest fire,
Gutting by its sparks,
The bunch of (tail) hair of Chamaris[160];
Should (such) a forest fire,
Ravage it (the Himālayās),
By the profusion of (your) water showers,
Dousing it completely,
Would be befitting for you;
The wealth of the righteous,
Indeed lies in the outcome,
Of alleviating the sufferings,
Of the distressed"[161]

ये संरम्भोत्पतनरभसाः स्वाङ्गभङ्गाय तस्मिन्
मुक्ताध्वानं सपदि शरभा लङ्घयेयुर्भवन्तम् ।
तान् कुर्वीथास्तुमुलकरकावृष्टिपातावकीर्णान्
के वा न स्युः परिभवपदं निष्फलारम्भयत्नाः ।।५८।।

Verse No. 58:

"On it (the Himālayās),
Are the Śarabhās,[162]
Who gallop in leaps and bounds;
Prodded by (their) (innate) impulses of rage;
Should they suddenly attack you[163],

[160] The Chamaris are a breed of deer which are like a cow in appearance; their tail hair are very delicate and easily combustible.

[161] This shows among the ethical values then prevalent in the Indian society benevolence was highly esteemed.

[162] The Śarabhās were a distinctive breed of eight-legged deer. They were known to kill even a tiger, their traditional enemy.

[163] Probably mistaking the Cloud for a tiger as per the Mahākavi.

(Though) out of (their) way,
(Only) to break their bodies,
(On crashing down);
By a heavy shower of hail stones,
Bring about their dispersal;
Whomsoever are engaged in futile efforts,
Cannot but become
An object of derision"

तत्र व्यक्तं दृषदि चरणन्यासमर्धेन्दुमौलेः
शश्वत्सिद्धैरुपचितबलिं भक्तिनम्रः परीयाः ।
यस्मिन् दृष्टे करणविगमादूर्ध्वमुद्धूतपापाः
कल्पिष्यन्ते स्थिरगणपदप्राप्तये श्रद्दधानाः ।।५९।।

Verse No. 59:

"On a certain stone slab there (Himālayās),
Visible is the imprint,
Of the foot of Śivaji,
(The God) (bearing) on (his) head the lunar crescent;
Circumambulate it,
Humble in faith;
Homage is paid,
Ritualistically to (this) footprint,
By the Siddhās[164],
At all times;
By having (merely) sighted it,
Those bereft of sin and endowed with faith,
Become worthy of attaining,
After having discarded their mortal frame,
The eternal abode of the Gaṇās[165]"

शब्दायन्ते मधुरमनिलैः कीचकाः पूर्यमाणाः
संरक्ताभिस्त्रिपुरविजयो गीयते किन्नरीभिः ।
निर्ह्रादस्ते मुरजे इव चेत् कन्दरेषु ध्वनिः स्यात्

[164] Siddhās are Yogis dedicated to Śivaji's worship.
[165] Ganās are counted among the supreme devotees of Śivaji.

संगीतार्थो ननु पशुपतेस्तत्र भावी समग्रः ।।६०।।

Verse No. 60:

"There (in the Himālayās),
Flutes made of bamboos,
Being filled with air,
Produce notes sweetly;
(Śivaji's) victory (song) over Tripura[166],
Being recited by the wives of Kinnaras[167],
So very fond of music;
Should in the (surrounding) caves,
Your (Oh ! Cloud) thunder appear,
As if being the notes,
(Produced) on Muraj[168];
Indeed (then) whatever is needed,
For Śivā's musical concert,
Would be at that place"

प्रालेयाद्रेरुपतटमतिक्रम्य तांस्तान् विशेषान्
हंसद्वारं भृगुपतियशोवर्त्म यत् क्रौञ्चरन्ध्रम् ।
तेनोदीचीं दिशमनुसरेस्तिर्यगायामशोभी
श्यामः पादो बलिनियमनाभ्युद्यतस्येव विष्णोः ।।६१।।

Verse No. 61:

"Having crossed all those memorable sites[169],
Close to the Himālayan plateau,
Follow the northerly direction;
Through an aperture in Kraunch mountain[170],
Which is the entrance for royal swans,

---

[166] A ferocious demon killed by Śivaji.

[167] Kinnaras are demigods with human figures but with the mouth of a horse.

[168] A special percussion instrument with resounding notes played during Śivaji's āarti to this day. This shows the unbroken tradition of Śivaji's ritualistic worship over the last two millennia.

[169] These are the sites alluded to in earlier verses.

[170] Paraśurāma had pierced a long hole through the Kraunch mountain, believed to be in the Himāchal Pradesh, while engaged in an archery competition with Kārttikeya.

(On way to the Mānas Sarovar);
Being (also) the path of fame,
Of Paraśurāma[171];
(You, Oh ! Cloud),
Looking attractive,
(Having adopted) length-wise a diagonal like posture[172],
Like the darkish foot of Lord Viṣnu,
While he was engaged,
In restraining (demon) Bali[173]"

गत्वा चोर्ध्वं दशमुखभुजोच्छ्वासितप्रस्थसंधेः
कैलासस्य त्रिदशवनितादर्पणस्यातिथिः स्याः ।
श्रृङ्गोच्छ्रायैः कुमुदविशदैर्यो वितत्य स्थितः खम्
राशीभूतः प्रतिदिनमिव त्र्यम्बकस्याट्टहासः ।।६२।।

Verse No. 62:

"[After traversing the aperture,
In the Kraunch mountain][174],
And having moved upwards,
Become the guest,
Of the Kailāś mountain;
(Verily) the mirror,
Of celestial damsels;
The joints of (whose) crests,
Were loosened by the (mighty) arms,
Of Rāvaṇa[175];
It (Kailāś) is there,
Encompassing the sky,
By the loftiness of its peaks,
Nothing but immaculate white lotuses;

---

[171] --ibid--

[172] To wriggle through a time aperture the Cloud had to squeeze himself.

[173] Lord Viṣnu had consigned the demon Bali to the netherworld by placing his foot in a slanting mode on his head while pushing him down. Hence such a simile by the Mahākavi.

[174] As referred in verse 61.

[175] This had happened when Rāvaṇa had made a futile effort to carry off Kailāś to Lankā

(The Kailāś mountain being),
Like the peals of laughter[176],
Of Śivaji,
Accumulated day after day"

उत्पश्यामि त्वयि तटगते स्निग्धभिन्नाञ्जनाभे
सद्यःकृत्तद्विरददशनच्छेदगौरस्य तस्य ।
शोभामद्रेः स्तिमितनयनप्रेक्षणीयां भवित्री–
मंसन्यस्ते सति हलभृतो मेचके वाससीव ।।६३।।

Verse No. 63:
"That snow-white mountain (Kailāś),
Being (like) a fragment,
Of a freshly - cut tusk of an elephant;
Yourself (Oh ! Cloud) (possessed) of gloss,
Of smoothly ground Kohl;
No sooner you attain its plateau,
I envisage,
Beauty of that mountain (Kailāś),
Would become worthy of being watched,
With unblinking gaze;
Like that of Balarāma[177],
With dark cloth on (his) shoulder"

हित्वा तस्मिन् भुजगवलयं शंभुना दत्तहस्ता
क्रीडाशैले यदि च विचरेत् पादचारेण गौरी ।
भङ्गीभक्त्या विरचितवपुः स्तम्भितान्तर्जलौघः
सोपानत्वं कुरु मणितटारोहणायाग्रयायी ।।६४।।

Verse No. 64:
"On that pleasure - mountain[178] (Kailāś),

---

[176] Śivaji's laughter is usually qualified as 'white' to connote it being free of malice and negative emotions.
[177] Balarāma was exceedingly fair. A parallel is therefore drawn by the Mahākavi between Balarāma with a dark cloth placed on his shoulder, and the snow-white Kailāś maintain topped by the dark cloud.

Should Gauriji amble on foot,
Having been offered (his) hand,
By Śivaji,
With (his) serpent-bracelet discarded[179];
Precede them (Oh ! Cloud),
Suppressing within you,
The flow of waters;
Transform (your) body,
Into a series of ascending curves;
(And) enact the role of a ladder,
(For the celestial couple),
To ascend to the bejewelled[180] plateau"

तत्रावश्यं वलयकुलिशोद्घट्टनोद्गीर्णतोयं,
नेष्यन्ति त्वां सुरयुवतयो यन्त्रधारागृहत्वम् ।
ताभ्यो मोक्षस्तव यदि सखे घर्मलब्धस्य न स्यात्,
क्रीडालोलाः श्रवणपरुषैर्गर्जितैर्भाययेस्ताः ।।६५।।

Verse No. 65:

"(Oh ! Cloud),
The celestial damsels there (on the Kailāś),
Will undoubtedly transform you,
Into a virtual shower-room[181],
With (yourself) oozing waters,
(After) being pummelled (by them),
With the hard points of (their) bracelets;
Oh ! friend !
If with yourself being in the midst of summer[182],

---

[178] The Kailāś mountain had been created by the Devās for the indulgence of Śivaji and Pārvatiji.
[179] This was to reassure Pārvatiji who was terrified of snakes.
[180] Kailāś was composed of jewels and gems.
[181] It would seem that shower-baths were in vogue even two millennia ago. So much for the so-called 'backwardness' of that era.
[182] The Cloud was expected to reach Kailāś during summer. It may be recalled that its journey had started during the previous monsoon. (Please see verse no.3). This was indeed a long journey from central India to north of the Himālayās.

No escape is there,
From them,
Frighten them away,
By (your) thunder,
Jarring to the ear![183]
They being fond of frolic"

हेमाम्भोजप्रसवि सलिलं मानसस्याददानः
कुर्वन् कामं क्षणमुखपटप्रीतिमैरावतस्य ।
धुन्वन्कल्पद्रुमकिसलयान्यंशुकानीव वातै-
र्नानाचेष्टैर्जलद ललितैर्निर्विशेस्तं नगेन्द्रम् ।।६६।।

Verse No. 66:
"Oh! Cloud (while on Kailāś),
Momentarily gratifying Airāvata[184],
By (covering his) face,
(As if by a) fabric;
While he is imbibing,
The waters of the Mānas Sarovar,
These being the source,
Of golden lotuses;
Ruffling by (your) air draughts,
The leaves of the Wish Tree,
Like delicate silken fabrics;
Indulge yourself (thus)[185],

---

183 The Yakśa obviously did not want the Cloud to remain entrapped by celestial damsels cooling them with his showers. Hence he suggested to him a means of escape.

184 Mahākavi envisages Airāvata coming over there to drink waters of the Mānas Sarovar. The Cloud being wet could momentarily cover Airāvata's face pleasing him.

185 This is an illustration of the close, loving relationship subsisting between the Cloud and the Kailaś mountain. Earlier too there have been many allusions regarding the intimate relationship of the Cloud with mountains, rivers, etc. The Mahākavi is thus projecting the unity of the ecosystem - a vital concept which alas was totally lost sight of over the centuries. As per Mallināth, the famous commentator on Meghadūt, the Himālaya was like the place of Cloud's in-laws. This was because the Ganges, the beloved of the Cloud, was Himālaya's

To your heart's content,
On that Lord of the mountains (the Himālayās),
By different activities,
Frolicsome and pleasurable"

तस्योत्सङ्गे प्रणयिन इव स्त्रस्तगङ्गादुकूलां
न त्वं दृष्ट्वा न पुनरलकां ज्ञास्यसे कामचारिन् ।
या वः काले वहति सलिलोद्गारमुच्चैर्विमाना
मुक्ताजालग्रथितमलकं कामिनीवाभ्रवृन्दम् ॥६७॥

Verse No. 67:
"Marked by towering mansions,
The Alakā (Nagari) [186],
(Nestles) in the lap of that lover (of hers),
(The Kailāś mountain);
The Ganges river,
Being as if (her) (Alakā Nagari's)
White silken upper garment,[187]
That has slipped down;
In your (favourite) season, Oh! Free-Wanderer, (Oh! Cloud),
(In the monsoon),
(The Alakā Nagari) which bears multitudes of clouds,
Spewing water,
Resembling a gentle and serene damsel,
(Her) hair interwoven with pearl-strings[188];
Having seen (once) the Alakā (Nagari),
No way can you then,
Not know it"

---

daughter. This is why the Mahākavi had advised the Cloud to feel at ease there and enjoy himself.

[186] Alakā is the fabled capital city of Kubera.

[187] Alakā is situated on the top of the Kailāś mountain. The Ganges with her sparkling white waters flows below. This is why a simile is drawn by the Mahākavi between the Ganges and a silken white upper garment of the beloved maiden that has dropped off.

[188] The pearl-strings correspond to rain waters while the dark clouds resemble the tresses.

The Meghādūtam
Uttarmegh

विद्युत्वन्तं ललितवनिताः सेन्द्रचापं सचित्राः
संगीताय प्रहतमुरजाः स्निग्धगम्भीरघोषम् ।
अन्तस्तोयं मणिमयभुवस्तुङ्गमभ्रंलिहाग्राः
प्रासादास्त्वां तुलयितुमलं यत्र तैस्तैर्विशेषैः ।।१।।

Verse No. 1:

"Where (in the Alakā[1] city),
There being mansions,
Having the (wherewithal) of rising to your standards,
Thanks to (their) this or that special feature;
Yourself flashing with lightning,
(While) glowing being the damsels of (those) mansions;
The (multi-hued) rainbow of yourself,
(Decorated) with pictures being the mansions;
Sonorous yet sweet thundering of yourself,
(But) striking of percussion instruments,
For concerts in mansions;
(Reservoir) of water within you,
Paved with gems,
Being the grounds of palaces;
With yourself soaring into the sky,
Abutting the heaven,
Being the mansions' uppermost portions"[2]

हस्ते लीलाकमलमलके बालकुन्दानुविद्धम्
नीता लोध्रप्रसवरजसा पाण्डुतामानने श्रीः ।
चूडापाशे नवकुरबकं चारु कर्णे शिरीषं
सीमन्ते च त्वदुपगमजं यत्र नीपं वधूनाम् ।।२।।

---

[1] Alakā is the legendary city of Kubera on the Kailaś mountain marked by unimaginable wealth and opulence. In the ensuing verses of this part II we will come across many many tantalizing descriptions of it.

[2] The Mahākavi clearly anticipated with his prescient imagination the building boom of the modern era.

Verse No. 2:

"Where (in the Alakā city),
In the hands of married ladies,
Are lotus flowers,
(Carried) for frolic;
(Their) hair being strung,
With Kunda blossom;
The charm on (their) visage,
Rendered into whitish tinge,
By the pollen,
Of Lodhra[3] flowers;
In the tresses,
Fresh Kurabak flowers;
The splendid Śiriş[4],
Being on the ear;
(And) in the parting of hair,
On (their) head,
Being Kadamb[5] flowers,
Springing forth in rainy days"

यत्रोन्मत्तभ्रमरमुखराः पादपा नित्यपुष्पाः,
हंसश्रेणीरचितरशना नित्यपद्मा नलिन्यः ।
केकोत्कण्ठा भवनशिखिनो नित्यभास्वत्कलापा
नित्यज्योत्स्ना प्रतिहततमोवृत्तिरम्याः प्रदोषाः ।।३।।

Verse No. 3:

"Wherein (in the Alakā city),
The trees there being ever flower bearing,

---

[3] Various flowers enumerated in this verse grow during different seasons. For example, the Lodhra flower grows in winter while the Kadamb flower appears in monsoon. By this the Mahākavi wishes to indicate that in the Alakā city all the seasons could be experienced at the same time -- such was its uniqueness and marvel.

[4] This is a very delicate flower which is typical of summer. It is a favourite of the Mahākavi and finds repeated mention in his texts.

[5] This verse also clearly brings out that even two millennia ago the ladies embellished themselves with flowers more or less the same way as they do now.

Noisy due to (humming) of bees,
Gone amuck;
Lakes with lotuses always blooming,
Circles of swans,
Arrayed (around them),
(Like) waistbands;
Domesticated peacocks (their) plumages ever radiant,
(Sweetly) cooing,
Being upraised of necks;
Delightful being the nights,
The envelope of darkness dissipated,
With the moon light eternally present"

आनन्दोत्त्थं नयनसलिलं यत्र नान्यैर्निमित्तै-
नर्न्यिस्तापः कुसुमशरजादिष्टसंयोगसाध्यात् ।
नाप्यन्यस्मात् प्रणयकलहाद्विप्रयोगपपत्ति-
र्वित्तेशानां न च खलु वयो यौवनादन्यदस्ति ।।४।।

Verse No. 4:

"Where (in that Alakā city),
For no cause whatsoever,
Except joyfulness,
Tears ever appear,
In the eyes of Lords of wealth;
(Verily) no mental agony for them,
Except when being the target,
(Of Cupid's) flowery arrow,
(Getting thus afflicted with the malady of love),
To be overcome,
Through the union with the loved one;
Except only out of love tiffs,
For them never any separation,
(From the loved ones);
For (these) Lords,
Truly there exists no phase of life,
(Perpetual) youthfulness apart"[6]

---

[6] What a fantastic portrayal of Utopia, wholly hedonistic and sensuous.

यस्यां यक्षाः सितमणिमयान्येत्य हर्म्यस्थलानि
ज्योतिश्छायाकुसुमरचितान्युत्तमस्त्रीसहायाः ।
आसेवन्ते मधु रतिफलं कल्पवृक्षप्रसूतं
त्वद्गम्भीरध्वनिषु शनकैः पुष्करेष्वाहतेषु ।।५।।

Verse No. 5:

"The palaces wherein (in the Alakā city),
Their top terraces paved with crystal,
(Bearing) the reflection of heavenly bodies,
(As if) being flower decorations (arrangements);
The Yakshās accompanied by beautiful women,
Having reached them (terraces),
Gingerly sip the exhilarating wine,[7]
Produced by the wish-fulfilling Tree;
While gently played are the drums,
(Emitting sounds resembling),
Your deep thunder"[8]

मन्दाकिन्याः सलिलशिशिरैः सेव्यमाना मरुद्भि-
र्मन्दाराणामनुतटरुहां छायया वारितोष्णाः ।
अन्वेष्टव्यैः कनकसिकतामुष्टिनिक्षेपगूढैः
संक्रीडन्ते मणिभिरमरप्रार्थिता यत्र कन्याः ।।६।।

Verse No. 6:

"(The Alakā city) where celestial maidens,
Solicited by gods,
Play about gingerly with gems,
To be searched for,
(After) having been concealed,
By (their) fists thrust into golden sands;
They being shielded from the heat,
By the shades,

---

[7] The Mahākavi here unabashedly emerges as an exponent of Charvakā's hedonism.

[8] The Mahākavi thus clearly delineates the three main ingredients of hedonism - wine, women and song.

Of Mandārā trees,
Having come up on the banks,
Of the river 'Mandākinī';[9]
The celestial maidens,
Being caressed by the breeze,
Cooled by its waters"[10]

नीवीबन्धोच्छ्वसितशिथिलं यत्र बिम्बाधराणाम्
क्षौमं रागादनिभृतकरेष्वाक्षिपत्सु प्रियेषु ।
अर्चिस्तुङ्गानभिमुखमपि प्राप्य रत्नप्रदीपान्
ह्रीमूढानां भवति विफलप्रेरणा चूर्णमुष्टिः ।।७।।

Verse No. 7:
"Where (in that city of Alakā),
As the lovers with restless hands,
Overwhelmed by passion,
Rip off the silk inner garment,
Being loose its knots unravelled,
Of (their beloved ladies);
With 'bimba' (like) lower lip,[11]
They turning witless out of modesty,[12]
(Fling fistful of powder,
Towards jewel-lamps);
(But) futile proves (their) effort,[13]
(Despite)(that) powder reaching the jewel-lamps,
Its rays of light shooting up"[14]

---

[9] The portion of the Gangā which flows through the heaven is called Mandākinī.

[10] The Alakā city is very much a part of the heaven. This is also borne out by the fact that the Mandākinī, the heavenly Ganges, flows through it.

[11] The bimba is a red fruit. This simile is usually used to describe the lips of a beautiful lady.

[12] The Mahākavi shows familiarity with female psychology which has presumably not changed over the centuries.

[13] The lamps were enkindled by gems. This is why dust could not extinguish them as would have happened in case of ordinary oil lamps. This shows that the gems in the Alakā city had amazing radiance and sparkle.

[14] --ibid--

नेत्रा नीताः सततगतिना यद्विमानाग्रभूमी-
रालेख्यानां स्वजलकणिकादोषमुत्पाद्य सद्यः ।
शङ्कास्पृष्टा इव जलमुचस्त्वादृशाः जालमार्गै-
र्धूमोद्गारानुकृतिनिपुणा जर्जरा निष्पतन्ति ॥८॥

Verse No. 8:

"(In the Alakā city),
The (clouds) like yourself,
Letting out water,
That are carried to the top terraces,
Of its seven-storied skyscrapers,[15]
By the agency (of the wind),
In steady motion;
Having caused damage,
By (their) water drops,
To the paintings (of the mansions),
Turning (then) apprehensive as it were,
Immediately stream out,
From the (escape) route,
(Provided) by (window) lattices,
Disintegrated and fragmented,
In veritable imitation,
Of smoke emissions"

यत्र स्त्रीणां प्रियतमभुजालिङ्गनोच्छ्वासिताना-
मङ्गग्लानिं सुरतजनितां तन्तुजालावलम्बाः ।
त्वत्संरोधापगमविशदैश्चन्द्रपादैर्निशीथे
व्यालुम्पन्ति स्फुटजललवस्यन्दिनश्चन्द्रकान्ताः ॥९॥

Verse No. 9:

"Where (in that Alakā city),
At midnight,
The Chandrakānt gems,
Hanging by the nets of thread,

---

[15] This is indicative of the fact that even during Mahakavi's period going back to two millennia high-rise structures were associated with opulence.

(Attached to the ceiling),
Oozing out pure water drops,[16]
(Being exposed) to the moon rays,
Clear due to disappearance,
Of your (Cloud's) covering;
These gems dispel,
The bodily languor of women,
Being the outcome of indulgence;
Having been held in embrace,
In the arms of their paramours,
Making them (thoroughly) relaxed"

अक्षय्यान्तर्भवननिधयः प्रत्यहं रक्तकण्ठै
रुद्गायद्भिर्धनपतियशः किन्नरैर्यत्र सार्धम् ।
वैभ्राजाख्यं विबुधवनितावारमुख्यासहाया
बद्धालापा बहिरुपवनं कामिनो निर्विशन्ति ॥१०॥

Verse No. 10:
"Where (in that Alakā city),
The lustful (Yakśās),
Inexhaustible being the treasures,
In (their) palaces,
Enjoy themselves every day,
In the outer garden,
Of (Alakā) called Vaibhrāja;
Engrossed in chatting,
(With) (their) companions,
The celestial damsels,
Best of courtesans;
In the company of Kinnars,
Engaged in loudly singing,
In a melodious voice,
The glory of Kubera."

[16] This expresses the belief then prevalent that pure water oozed out of moon gems when exposed to moon rays.

गत्युत्कम्पादलकपतितैर्यत्र मन्दारपुष्पैः
पत्रच्छेदैः कनककमलैः कर्णविभ्रंशिभिश्च ।
मुक्ताजालैः स्तनपरिसरच्छिन्नसूत्रैश्च हारै–
नैंशो मार्गः सवितुरुदये सूच्यते कामिनीनाम् ।।११।।

Verse No. 11:
"Where (in the city of Alakā),
The path of courting damsels,
(Treaded on) in the night,
Is pointed out on sun rise,
By the Mandāra flowers,
Dropped off from (their) hair;
And by the golden lotuses,
Petals fragmented,
Fallen from (their) ears;
(And by the pearls),
(Dropped off) from pearl strings,[17]
(As well as by fallen flowers),
(From the) garlands,
With their threads torn,
In the region of (madens') breasts;
(All this)
Due to swaying and shaking,
(of their bodies),[18]
Thanks to rapid gait"[19]

वासश्चित्रं मधु नयनयोर्विभ्रमादेशदक्षं,
पुष्पोम्देदं सह किसलयैर्भूषणानां विकल्पान् ।
लाक्षारागं चरणकमलन्यासयोग्यं च यस्या–
मेकः सूते सकलमबलामण्डनं कल्पवृक्षः ।।१२।।

---

[17] Worn around the head
[18] These ladies are anxious to meet their lovers. With unsteady, rapid gait they are rushing to them. As a result flowers, golden lotuses, etc., fall off from their bodies.
[19] --ibid--

Verse No. 12:

"(In the city of Alakā) wherein,
The 'Wishing Tree' by itself alone,
Produces the embellishments in entirety,
Of the ladies (such as),
Multi-hued fabrics;
(And) wine which is unfaltering,
In its guidance to the eyes,
Towards coquetry;
(As well as),
Sprouts along with blooming flowers;
Varieties of ornaments;
And dye-lac appropriate for application,
To (their) lotus (like) feet"

पत्रश्यामा दिनकरहयस्पर्धिनो यत्र वाहाः
शैलोदग्रास्त्वमिव करिणो वृष्टिमन्तः प्रभेदात् ।
योधाग्रण्यः प्रतिदशमुखं संयुगे तस्थिवांसः
प्रत्यादिष्टाभरणरुचयश्चन्द्रहासव्रणाङ्कैः ॥१३॥

Verse No. 13:

"It is where (in Alakā),
Horses darkish-green (in hue) (like) leaves,
Being competitors (in speed),
With the Sun's horses;
Mountain (like) towering elephants,
With ichor streaming out,[20]
Showering rains,
Resembling you (the Cloud);
Leading warriors,
Who had remained unflinching,
In face-to-face battle,
With Rāvana;
Having abjured (their) love of ornaments,
Thanks to the scars,

[20] Powerful elephants are usually portrayed in Sanskrit literature as marked by flowing ichor. No doubt, in those pristine times horses, elephants and even men were far stronger than what they are today.

Made by the sword of Rāvana,[21]"

मत्वा देवं धनपतिसखं यत्र साक्षाद् वसन्तं
प्रायश्चापं न वहति भयान्मन्मथः षट्पदज्यम् ।
सभ्रूभङ्गप्रहितनयनैः कामिलक्ष्येष्वमोघै-
स्तस्यारम्भश्चतुरवनिताविभ्रमैरेव सिद्धः ॥१४॥

Verse No. 14:

"Being aware that is where (in Alakā) resides,
God (Śivaji) himself, friend of Kubera,
The God of Love often does not wield,
Being apprehensive,[22]
(His) bow with bees for the string;
(But) his mission is very much fulfilled,
By damsels conversant with ways of the world,
Through coquetry,
Glancing (alluringly) with eyebrows knitted,
Never failing to reach,
The intended lover"

तत्रागारं धनपतिगृहानुत्तरेणास्मदीयं
दूराल्लक्ष्यं सुरपतिधनुश्चारुणा तोरणेन ।
यस्योपान्ते कृतकतनयः कान्तया वर्धितो मे,
हस्तप्राप्यस्तबकनमितो बालमन्दारवृक्षः ॥१५॥

Verse No. 15:

"There (in the Alakā nagari),
Very close to Kubera's palace,
To the north,
Is the mansion of ours,
Observable from afar,
By (its) dazzling arched gateway,

---

[21] Rāvana, a great devotee of Śivaji, had once tried to carry away the Kailas mountain to Lanka. This was resisted by Śivaji and his cohort. Thus a battle had ensued between the warriors in Alakā and Rāvana.

[22] It is well known that the God of love is very much afraid of Śivaji who had in wrath reduced him to ashes by opening his third eye.

(Like) Indra's bow;
In its proximity,
Nurtured by my beloved wife,
Like a foster-son,
Being a small Mandār tree,
Bending with (flower) bunches,
(Easily) reachable by hand"

वापी चास्मिन् मरकतशिलाबद्धसोपानमार्गा,
हैमैश्छन्ना विकचकमलैः स्निग्धवैदूर्यनालैः ।
यस्यास्तोये कृतवसतयो मानसं सन्निकृष्टं
नाध्यास्यन्ति व्यपगतशुचस्त्वामपि प्रेक्ष्य हंसाः ।।१६।।

Verse No. 16:

"Moreover in it (in Yakśā's palace),
Is a pond,
Covered by blooming lotuses wrought of gold,
(Their) stalks (crafted) of smooth Vaidūrya stones,
The path (to it),
Being a flight of steps,
Created out of emerald stones;
The swans residing in its waters,
Even (after) having observed you,
Remain unconcerned;[23]
(And) do not long,
For the 'Mānas' Sarovar,
Nearby as it is"[24] [25]

---

[23] The swans are fully assured that the waters of the pond will forever remain absolutely pure, no matter what. This is why even after observing the Cloud overhead, in no way they worry that its waters will pollute the pond.

[24] The Mahākavi here is emphasizing the extraordinary purity of the pond in Yakśā's palace. This is why the swans there have no particular desire to move on to the Mānas Sarovar, though nearby.

[25] The Mahākavi has indirectly implied that the pond in Yakśā's palace rivaled in purity the legendary Mānas sarovar. Through this metaphor he has emphasized in the strongest possible way the grandeur of Yakśā's residence.

तस्यास्तीरे रचितशिखरः पेशलैरिन्द्रनीलैः
क्रीडाशैलः कनककदलीवेष्टनप्रेक्षणीयः ।
मद्गेहिन्याः प्रिय इति सखे चेतसा कातरेण
प्रेक्ष्योपान्तस्फुरिततडितं त्वां तमेव स्मरामि ॥१७॥

Verse No. 17:

"On its (pond's) side,
Is a spectacular pleasure-mountain,
Having been encircled,
By plantain trees wrought of gold;
The mountain's peak,
Created out of charming 'Indraneel' gems;
Favourite of my wife,
(Being that mountain);
Oh ! friend,
With an agitated mind,[26]
I (the Yakśa) am reminded of that only,[27]
Having observed you hither,
With flashes of lightning"

रक्ताशोकश्चलकिसलयः केसरश्चात्रकान्तः,
प्रत्यासन्नौ कुरबकवृतेर्माधवीमण्डपस्य ।
एकः सख्यास्तव सह मया वामपादाभिलाषी,
काङ्क्षत्यन्यो वदनमदिरां दोहदच्छद्मनाऽस्याः ॥१८॥

Verse No. 18:

"There (on the pleasure mountain),
In proximity to a bower,
Of Mādhavi (creepers),
Hedged by Kurbak trees,
Is a red Aśoka (tree),
Of swaying leaves,

---

[26] The pleasure-mountain covered by golden plantain trees has a scintillating appearance. The Cloud marked by flashes of lightning therefore reminds the Yakśa of that only. His mind therefore becomes agitated as the pleasure-mountain was much liked by his wife.
[27] --ibid--

As well as a charming Kesara (tree);
Under the pretext of Dohada,[28]
Craves one (of them), (the Aśoka),
(To be struck) in my company,
By the left foot of your friend,
[Yakśa's wife];
(While) the other longs for,
Her mouthful of wine,[29]
(To be spit on it)"

तन्मध्ये च स्फटिकफलका काञ्चनी वासयष्टि-
मूले बद्धा मणिभिरनतिप्रौढवंशप्रकाशैः ।
तालैः शिञ्जावलयसुभगैर्नर्तितः कान्तया मे,
यामध्यास्ते दिवसविगमे नीलकण्ठः सुहृद्वः ।।१९।।

Verse No. 19:
"And[30] there is a perch of gold,
Between them (the Aśoka and Kesara trees),[31]
With a crystal platform,
Stabilized on a foundation,
By gems,
Of (hue) like that of young bamboo shoots;
On the perch,
Roosts a peacock[32]
Your (Oh ! Cloud) friend,
At end of the day;

---

[28] Here the Mahākavi has referred to Dohada, a superstitious belief then prevailing. As per it, trees blossomed when struck by the left foot of a damsel in the company of her husband or after she spitted out a mouthful of wine on it. Both the trees are tempting the Yakśiṇi to perform 'Dohada' so that they blossom. There are also repeated references to 'Dohada' and how its performance led to flowering of the Aśoka tree in Mahakavi's famous drama Mālvikāgnimitram.

[29] This shows wine drinking by ladies was a socially acceptable practice during Mahākavi's era.

[30] The word 'and' connotes continuation of the description of the pleasure mountain given in verse no.17.

[31] These trees have been referred to the earlier verse no. 18.

[32] A close loving bond is presupposed between peacocks and clouds with the former becoming exuberant by the latter.

Made to dance by my wife,
By the rhythmic clapping,
Of (her) hands,
Rendered pleasing,
By the jingling of (her) bangles"

एभिः साधो हृदयनिहितैर्लक्षणैर्लक्षयेथा
द्वारोपान्ते लिखितवपुषौ शङ्खपद्मौ च दृष्ट्वा ।
क्षामच्छायं भवनमधुना मद्वियोगेन नूनं
सूर्यापाये न खलु कमलं पुष्यति स्वामभिख्याम् ॥२०॥

Verse No. 20:

"Oh ! knowledgeable (Cloud),
Undoubtedly will you identify,
(My) mansion,
By these distinguishing features,[33]
(Which) have been embedded in (your) heart;
As well as by observing,
On either sides of its door,
Painted figures of Śankha and Padma;
Verily then in gloom,
In my absence,
Would be (that) mansion;
A lotus truly does not,
Assume its own charm,
On setting of the sun"[34]

गत्वा सद्यः कलभतनुतां शीघ्रसम्पातहेतोः
क्रीडाशैले प्रथमकथिते रम्यसानौ निषण्णः ।
अर्हस्यन्तर्भवनपतितां कर्तुमल्पाल्पभासं,
खद्योतालीविलसितनिभां विद्युदुन्मेषदृष्टिम् ॥२१॥

---

[33] The same have been portrayed in earlier stanzas 15, 16, 17, 18 and 19.

[34] In this metaphor the sun is compared to the Yakśa (master of the house); in their absence both the lotus (the sun's lover) and the house become listless.

Verse No. 21:

"(Says Yakśa continuing his advice),
(After) having reached (my mansion),
For the sake of a quick access (into it),
(Adopt) at once a tiny body,
Like that of a baby elephant;[35]
(And) be seated,
On the beautiful peak,
Of the pleasure-mountain,[36]
Portrayed earlier;[37]
Make (your) gaze,
Being flashes of lightning,
Descending into (my) residence,
Of very, very low luminosity,
Like that of a row,
Of glittering night flies"[38]

तन्वी श्यामा शिखरिदशना पक्वबिम्बाधरोष्ठी
मध्ये क्षामा चकितहरिणीप्रेक्षणा निम्ननाभिः ।
श्रोणीभारादलसगमना स्तोकनम्रा स्तनाभ्याम्,
या तत्र स्याद्युवतिविषये सृष्टिराद्येव धातुः ।।२२।।

Verse No. 22:

"(Describing the appearance of his wife,
The Yakśa narrates),[39]
The damsel who would be there,
(In my mansion),
Being youthful and slim,

---

[35] The Yakśa counsels the Cloud to become like a baby elephant in shape so that he can inconspicuously look into his house. Moreover it may be because both the elephant and the Cloud are dark in colour.

[36] The Cloud is advised to sit on a nearby peak of the pleasure mountain so that he could easily observe from the height the goings - on inside Yakśa's mansion.

[37] See verse no. 17.

[38] The Cloud is advised to avoid a bright glare and cast the soft light of fire-flies in order not to suddenly startle Yakśa's wife.

[39] The Yakśa had first depicted the prominent features of his palace so that the Cloud could easily locate it. Next he elaborates his wife's charming looks so that she could be identified by the Cloud.

With pointed teeth,[40]
Lower lip (like) a ripe bimba (fruit),[41]
Slender in the middle,
Eyes (like) a startled doe,[42]
Deep of naval,[43]
Slow of gait due to heaviness of hips,[44]
Learning forward a little,
Due to (expansive) breasts;[45]
As if she happens to be,[46]
The very first creation,
Among the female species
Of the creator"

तां जानीथाः परिमितकथां जीवितं मे द्वितीयम्
दूरीभूते मयि सहचरे चक्रवाकीमिवैकाम् ।
गाढोत्कण्ठां गुरुषु दिवसेष्वेषु गच्छत्सु बालां
जातां मन्ये शिशिरमथितां पद्मिनीं वाऽन्यरूपाम् ।।२३।।

Verse No. 23:
"Consider her (Oh ! Cloud),
(The damsel in the mansion),
Talking but little,
To be the second life of mine;[47]
With myself, her companion, far away,
Being like a Chakravakī,[48]
All by herself;

---

[40] Married ladies (with pointed teeth) were considered fortunate for their husbands.
[41] Widely used simile in Sanskrit literature for the portrayal of a beautiful damsel.
[42] --ibid--
[43] These show how the criteria and benchmarks of female beauty have changed over the centuries.
[44] --ibid--
[45] --ibid--
[46] This damsel is none but Yakśa's wife. This becomes clear in the next verse.
[47] Alludes to Yakśa.
[48] This is a proverbial love couple of Sanskrit. The female bird (Chakravakī) pitifully warbles whole night believing her companion, the male bird, to be away.

The hapless maiden,
Full of longings,
With the passage of these days,
Prolonged (due to anguish of separation),
I suspect,[49]
Has become of changed appearance,
Like a lotus,
Wilting in winter"

नूनं तस्याः प्रबलरुदितोच्छूननेत्रं प्रियाया
निःश्वासानामशिशिरतया भिन्नवर्णाधरोष्ठम् ।
हस्तन्यस्तं मुखमसकलव्यक्ति लम्बालकत्वा-
दिन्दोर्दैन्यं त्वदनुसरणक्लिष्टकान्तेर्बिभर्ति ।।२४।।

Verse No. 24:

"That darling[50] (of mine),[51]
With eyes swollen by inconsolable weeping;
The colour of lower lip changed,
Due to warmth of the sighs;[52]
The face not fully visible,
Placed on (her) hands,
(And) by long tresses (hanging loose),[53]
Indeed, her face projects a listless look,
(Like) that of the moon,
Its brightness obscured,
By your (Cloud's) cover"

आलोके ते निपतति पुरा सा बलिव्याकुला वा
मत्सादृश्यं विरहतनु वा भावगम्यं लिखन्ती ।
पृच्छन्ती वा मधुरवचनां सारिकां पञ्जरस्थां

[49] Alludes to Yakśa.
[50] Refers to Yakśa's wife.
[51] Refers to Yakśa.
[52] A distressed person sighs deeply and exhalations are warm.
[53] A chaste married woman whose husband was away was expected not to apply oil, etc., to her hair or to tie them up properly. This is why tresses were covering Yakśini's face. This theme has occurred many times in this lyric.

कच्चिद्भर्तुः स्मरसि रसिके त्वं हि तस्य प्रियेति ।।२५।।

Verse No. 25:

"Soon she[54] would come,
Into the range of your[55] sight;
Perhaps engaged in acts of worship;[56]
Or drawing a likeness of myself,
Having imagined (my) emaciated self,
Due to separation;
Or enquiring thus,
From the sweet talking, caged canary,
O joyful one : do you ever remember,
The Master (of yours),
Truly his loved one being yourself"

उत्सङ्गे वा मलिनवसने सौम्य निक्षिप्य वीणां
मद्गोत्राङ्कं विरचितपदं गेयमुद्गातुकामा ।
तन्त्रीमार्द्रां नयनसलिलैः सारयित्वा कथञ्चित्
भूयो भूयः स्वयमपि कृतां मूर्च्छनां विस्मरन्ती ।।२६।।

Verse No. 26:

"(Continuing the depiction,
Of his beloved's actions,[57]
The Yakśa goes on to say),
Oh ! gentle one,
Or else[58] somehow having wiped the Veena,[59]
Wet with (her)[60] tears,
Placing it on (her) lap,
Having wrap around of a dirty garment;[61]

---

[54] The word 'she' connotes Yakśa's wife.

[55] Here the Cloud is referred too. The Yakśa is saying that as the Cloud looks into his mansion (verse no. 21) his sight would fall upon his wife.

[56] To pray for Yakśa's safe and early return.

[57] The Yakśa is describing how his wife would be performing various actions such as engaging in worship, making his drawing, etc.

[58] --ibid--

[59] Veena is regarded as the oldest musical instrument of India. This reference shows it was played at least two thousand years ago.

[60] Here the Yakśa's wife is referred to.

Desirous of reciting a melody,
In a high-pitched tone,
Myself being the centre-piece,
Of the phrases composed;
(But) forgetting again and again,
The cadence of the notes,
Though herself having strung them together"

शेषान् मासान् विरहदिवसस्थापितस्यावधेर्वा
विन्यस्यन्ती भुवि गणनया देहलीदत्तपुष्पैः ।
मत्सङ्गं वा हृदयनिहितारम्भमास्वादयन्ती
प्रायेणैते रमणविरहेष्वङ्गनानां विनोदाः ।।२७।।

Verse No. 27:
"Or[62] she[63] enumerates,
The months remaining,
Of the period[64] prescribed,
From the day of separation,
By means of flowers on the threshold,
(Appropriately) arranging them on ground;[65]
Or she (mentally) keeps on relishing,
(The remembrances) of (amorous) acts,
(Performed) in my company,
Embedded in (her)[66] heart;
Usually these being the diversions,
Of ladies
During the separation

---

[61] Chaste wives whose husbands were away were expected to be unconcerned with their appearance.
[62] In this verse a survey of how Yakśa's wife would be occupying herself continues. See earlier verses nos. 25, 26.
[63] The allusion is to Yakśa's wife.
[64] This is the period of the curse during which the Yakśa was required to be away from Alakāpuri.
[65] The Yakśa's wife had probably kept 12 flowers on the thresh hold corresponding to the twelve months of separation. With the passage of each month, she would keep one flower on the ground, thus telling her at a glance how many months were left.
[66] The Yakśa's wife is referred to.

From their lover"[67]

सव्यापारामहनि न तथा पीडयेद्विप्रयोगः,
शङ्के रात्रौ गुरुतरशुचं निर्विनोदां सखीं ते ।
मत्सन्देशैः सुखयितुमलं पश्य साध्वीं निशीथे,
तामुन्निद्रामवनिशयनां सौधवातायनस्थः ।।२८।।

Verse No. 28:

"During the day,
Engaged in this activity or that,[68]
Separation doesn't distress your friend,[69]
In the same way,
As, I think, in the night,
With (her) anguish being greater,
Without any diversion;
(With yourself),
Perched on mansion's window,
Look at that poor lady,
Sleepless at midnight,
The resting place nothing but ground;[70]
Make her quite happy,
(By giving) my message"

आधिक्षामां विरहशयने सन्निषण्णैकपार्श्वां
प्राचीमूले तनुमिव कलामात्रशेषां हिमांशोः ।
नीता रात्रिः क्षण इव मया सार्धमिच्छारतैर्या
तामेवोष्णैर्विरहमहतीमश्रुभिर्यापयन्तीम् ।।२९।।

---

[67] How different is the present generation of ladies from those of ancient era. Is it truly a sign of progress?

[68] This refers to various actions like counting the months of separation left, making a painting of the Yakśa, etc. with which the Yakśa's wife kept herself busy during the day. See verses nos. 25, 26, 27.

[69] The phrase 'your friend' refers to Yakśa's wife. This phrase is used as the Yakśa' regards the Cloud as his friend.

[70] A married woman whose husband was away was expected sleep on bare ground.

Verse No. 29:

"(Oh ! Cloud ! observe my beloved),
Emaciated by mental agony,
Lying (inertly) like a figurine,
On her one side,
(Like) a single digit of the moon,
On the eastern horizon;
(Her) bed (nothing but ground covered only
with leaves, etc.),
(As befitting) a married lady,
Separated from her husband;[71]
The night that was passed,
As if being a moment,
In my company in love-making,
As per (her) wishes;[72]
Spending that only (now),
As if prolonged,
By the (anguish) of separation,
(Drenched) in hot tears"

पादानिन्दोरमृतशिशिराञ्जालमार्गप्रविष्टान्,
पूर्वप्रीत्या गतमभिमुखं सन्निवृत्तं तथैव ।
चक्षुःखेदात् सलिलगुरुभिः पक्ष्मभिश्छादयन्तीं,
साभ्रेऽह्नीव स्थलकमलिनीं न प्रबुद्धां न सुप्ताम् ॥३०॥

Verse No. 30:

"(My beloved),[73]
Out of fond (associations) of the past,[74]
(Her) eye(s) turning towards moon rays,
Soothing like nectar,
Streaming through the pathway,

---

[71] --ibid--

[72] This shows how in that era the woman's desires were given overwhelming importance even during moments of intimacy.

[73] The Yakśa continues to narrate to the Cloud the likely pathetic appearance of his beloved wife as the latter would find her. See earlier verses from 25 to 29.

[74] In the company of the Yakśa, the moon light was a source of great joy to the Yakśiṇi.

Of window lattices;
(But) in the very same way,
(Her) gaze withdrawn (quickly),
(Having remembered her separation);
Enveloping the (eyes') by eyelids,
Overflowing with tears,
Due to their (eyes) anguish;[75]
Like a lotus,
On a cloudy day,
Neither fully opened up,
Nor totally closed up"[76]

निःश्वासेनाधरकिसलयक्लेशिना विक्षिपन्तीं
शुद्धस्नानात् परुषमलकं नूनमागण्डलम्बम् ।
मत्सम्भोगः कथमुपनयेत् स्वप्नजोऽपीति निद्रा-
माकाङ्क्षन्तीं नयनसलिलोत्पीडरुद्धावकाशाम् ।।३१।।

Verse No. 31:
"(Observe my beloved),
(Her) rough hair very much dangling on the cheeks,[77]
Due to bathing only in water;[78]
They (hair) being blown sideways,
By sighs chafing the petal (like) lower lip;
Craving for sleep,
Lest at least dreaming,
Somehow or the other,
Would be experienced the union,

---

[75] Moon rays now remind her of the absence of the Yakśa causing acute agony. Tears therefore well up in her eyes and naturally the eyelashes flap down. This is a vivid and very realistic portrayal of how a lonely wife separated from her beloved husband would react. It highlights Mahakavi's power of minute observation.

[76] The lotus needs sunlight to bloom. When there is no sun as on a cloudy day it wilts. This is a metaphor for the Yakśa (the sun) and his wife (the lotus).

[77] Married women, husbands being away, were called upon to observe certain austerities as per the Śastrās and these included not applying oil to hair, not combing them, etc. This is why their hair lost smoothness and would become rough and unkempt.

[78] --ibid--

With me (by her);
(But) its (of sleep's) prospects dimmed,
By the torment caused,
By the (gushing) of tears,
From the eyes"[79]

आद्ये बद्धा विरहदिवसे या शिखा दाम हित्वा
शापस्यान्ते विगलितशुचा तां मयोद्वेष्टनीयाम् ।
स्पर्शक्लिष्टामयमितनखेनासकृत् सारयन्तीं
गण्डाभोगात् कठिनविषमामेकवेणीं करेण ।।३२।।

Verse No. 32:
"(These) tresses,
Which were tied up,
On the first day of separation,
After discarding of flower garlands;
That single braid of hair,
Unpleasant to touch, rough and jumbled up,
(My beloved)[80] pushing it away,
Repeatedly from the expanse of (her) cheeks,[81]
By (her) hand with unpared nails[82];
To be untwisted by me,
All angst gone,
On termination of the curse"

सा संन्यस्ताभरणमबला पेशलं धारयन्ती
शय्योत्सङ्गे निहितमसकृद् दुःखदुःखेन गात्रम् ।
त्वामप्यस्रं नवजलमयं मोचयिष्यत्यवश्यं,
प्रायः सर्वो भवति करुणावृत्तिरार्द्रान्तरात्मा ।।३३।।

---

[79] The Yakśa continues to describe the torments suffered by his wife in his absence; See earlier verses nos. 26 onwards.

[80] Here the Yakśa is continuing the narration of his wife's pitiful looks. The reference is therefore to the Yakśīṇī.

[81] The hair being unkempt tumble down on the cheeks.

[82] When the husband was away, the wife was expected to be unconcerned with her appearance; nails were therefore then not cut by such ladies.

Verse No. 33:

"She, the wife[83] (of mine),
Much worn down in body and spirit,
Bearing (her) delicate body,
Its embellishments discarded,
In extreme agony,
Having repeatedly placed it,
On the bed's middle;
She will necessarily,
Even[84] make you,
Shed tears of fresh water;
All with a soft heart,[85]
Usually turn out to be compassionate by nature"

जाने सख्यास्तव मयि मनः सम्भृतस्नेहमस्मा-
दित्थंभूतां प्रथमविरहे तामहं तर्कयामि ।
वाचालं मां न खलु सुभगंमन्यभावः करोति
प्रत्यक्षं ते निखिलमचिराद् भ्रातरुक्तं मया यत् ।।३४।।

Verse No. 34:

"Aware as I am[86],
That the mind of your friend[87],
Is full of love of me[88];
Out of (such exceeding love)
Have I portrayed,
Her[89] in this manner
During the first separation,
(Of ours);
Indeed, it is not (merely) envisaging,
Of (my) good fortune[90],

---

[83] This refers to the Yakśiṇī who is in a very poor condition due to the separation from the Yakśa.
[84] The word 'even' is used probably because the Cloud being insentient could be presumed to lack human feelings like pity.
[85] This literally applies to the Cloud as its interior consists of water.
[86] Refers to the Yakśa.
[87] Reference is to Yakśiṇi.
[88] Allusion to the Yakśa.
[89] The Yakśiṇi is indicated.

Which makes me talkative;
Oh ! Brother[91],
What has been said by me,
No sooner would be actually observed,
In entirety by you"

रुद्धापाङ्गप्रसरमलकैरञ्जनस्नेहशून्यं
प्रत्यादेशादपि च मधुनो विस्मृतभ्रूविलासम् ।
त्वय्यासन्ने नयनमुपरिस्पन्दि शङ्के मृगाक्ष्या
मीनक्षोभाच्चलकुवलयश्रीतुलामेष्यतीति ।।३५।।

Verse No. 35:
"The eye(s) of,
The doe-eyed (beloved of mine)[92],
With sideways glances obstructed,
By locks (tumbling down)[93];
The eye(s) bereft of smoothness,
(Lacking) collyrium;
And even oblivious of coquetry of eyebrows,
Out of abjuring of wine;
With you in proximity,
Upper part of the (left) eye throbbing;
I suspect it attaining thus,
The charm resembling that
Of a lotus,
(Displaying) rocking movement,
Thanks to the ripples caused by fish"

वामश्चास्याः कररुहपदैर्मुच्यमानो मदीयै–
र्मुक्ताजालं चिरपरिचितं त्याजितो दैवगत्या ।
संभोगान्ते मम समुचितो हस्तसंवाहनानां,
यास्यत्यूरुः सरसकदलीस्तम्भगौरश्चलत्वम् ।।३६।।

---

[90] By 'good fortune' the Yakśa implies having such a devoted wife.
[91] The Cloud is alluded to.
[92] The Yakśa here is narrating about the appearance of his wife.
[93] Since no oil was applied, the Yakśiṇi's hair was unkempt and therefore it would fall down on her face.

Verse No. 36:

"Her (of my beloved's)[94] left thigh,
Becoming bereft of my nailmarks,
Being like a whitish ripe stem of a plantain tree;
The pearl string long-accustomed,
(Around the waist),
Being divested,
As decreed by fate;
The thigh being eminently suitable,
In the aftermath of lovemaking,
For my hand caresses;
(With you[95] hovering nearby),
It will begin to pulsate[96]"

तस्मिन्काले जलद यदि सा लब्धनिद्रासुखा स्या-
दन्वास्यैनां स्तनितविमुखो याममात्रं सहस्व ।
मा भूदस्याः प्रणयिनि मयि स्वप्नलब्धे कथञ्चित्
सद्यः कण्ठच्युतभुजलताग्रन्थि गाढोपगूढम् ॥३७॥

Verse No. 37:

"Oh ! Cloud !
If she (my beloved) at that time[97]
Is relishing the pleasure of sleep,
(Then) perched behind her,
Wait for an hour or so,
Without thundering;
(Lest) having somehow or other,
In dream got hold of me,
Her paramour,

---

[94] The Yakśa is referring to his wife. He continues to describe her reaction as the Cloud approaches. See earlier stanza no. 35.

[95] This alludes to the Cloud.

[96] Pulsating of the left thigh was deemed to be an auspicious omen like throbbing of the left eye for a married lady.

[97] This is with reference to the preceding two stanzas, 35 and 36. The Yakśa narrated in them how the Yakśiṇi would react when she discovered that the Cloud was nearby.

The tight embrace (of hers),
With the enveloping of vine-like arms,
Suddenly does not fall apart,
At the throat"

तामुत्थाप्य स्वजलकणिकाशीतलेनानिलेन,
प्रत्याश्वस्तां सममभिनवैर्जालकैर्मालतीनाम् ।
विद्युद्गर्भः स्तिमितनयनां त्वत्सनाथे गवाक्षे
वक्तुं धीरः स्तनितवचनैर्मानिनीं प्रक्रमेथाः ।।३८।।

Verse No. 38:
"Waking her[98] (gently) up,
By the breeze,
Cooled by (your) own water drops;
Being reassured,
By means of,
Fresh buds of Mālatī flowers;
With yourself perched on the window,
Having become steadfast (and) with lightning shielded[99] within,
Be all set to address (my beloved)[100],
Self-respecting and looking amazed[101],
Through words being (verily),
(Nothing but your) thunder"

भर्तुर्मित्रं प्रियमविधवे विद्धिमामम्बुवाहं,
तत्सन्देशैर्हृदयनिहितैरागतं त्वत्समीपम् ।
यो वृन्दानि त्वरयति पथि श्राम्यतां प्रोषितानां
मन्द्रस्निग्धैर्ध्वनिभिरबलावेणिमोक्षोत्सुकानि ।।३९।।

---

[98] This refers to Yakśiṇi. In the last stanza (no. 37) she is described as being possibly asleep. The Yakśa is therefore explaining how she is to be aroused.
[99] To avoid frightening the Yakśiṇi with its bright glare.
[100] This refers to the Yakśiṇi.
[101] The amazement arises because the Yakśiṇi had no foreknowledge of Cloud's arrival.

Verse No. 39:

"Oh ! The one blessed with a husband,[102]
Know me, the water carrier,
As the dear friend of (your) Lord;
Having come near you,
(Bearing) his message,
Embedded in heart;
(I am the one),
Who hastens on (their) way,
By sweet (yet) grave sounds,
The groups of wearied travelers,
Eager to untwist,[103]
The braids of (their) miserable[104] loved ones"

इत्याख्याते पवनतनयं मैथिलीवोन्मुखी सा
त्वामुत्कण्ठोच्छ्वसितहृदया वीक्ष्य सम्भाव्य चैव ।
श्रोष्यत्यस्मात् परमवहिता सौम्य सीमन्तिनीनां
कान्तोदन्तः सुहृदुपनतः सङ्गमात् किञ्चिदूनः ॥४०॥

Verse No. 40:

"Having said this,[105]
She (my beloved),
(After) having observed you,[106]
And honoured you,
(Becoming) attentive would very much listen,
To what follows,
With her face upturned,
Chest heaving with eagerness;
As Sitādevi (had done),
Towards Hanuman, the son of wind;

---

[102] The Cloud thus reassures the anxious Yakśiṇi right at the outset about the well-being of her husband.

[103] The wives in that era tied up their hair prior to the departure of their husbands. The braid would be loosened only by the husband on his return.

[104] The wives would be most miserable in the absence of their husbands. This is the connotation of the word 'Abalā'.

[105] That the Cloud was the friend of Yakśiṇi's Lord.

[106] "You" alludes to the Cloud.

(This is because),
Oh ! gentle one,[107]
Tidings of the husband,
Brought by (his) friend,
Are only a little less (pleasing),
Than the union with him"[108]

तामायुष्मन् ! मम च वचनादात्मनश्चोपकर्तुं
ब्रूया एवं तव सहचरो रामगिर्याश्रमस्थः ।
अव्यापन्नः कुशलमबले पृच्छति त्वां वियुक्तः
पूर्वाभाष्यं सुलभविपदां प्राणिनामेतदेव ॥४१॥

Verse No. 41:
"Oh! long-lived one[109],
[110]And as per my words,
As well as doing a good turn to yourself,[111]
Convey the following,
To her[112] (my beloved);[113]
Your companion,[114]
Resident of the Rāmgiri hermitage,
(Suffering from agony) of separation,
(But still) alive;
Oh ! delicate one,
Enquires about (your) well-being;
This is what only,
Needs to be enquired first,

---

[107] This refers to the Cloud.

[108] This is reflective of the deep bonds of love which prevailed in that era between the husband and wife. It is evident from what has preceded that the husbands treated their wives with every consideration. Thus, to ensure the dignity of women their economic independence is far from essential as is believed almost axiomatically in present times, and has become a credo of modern civilization.

[109] Here the Cloud is referred to.

[110] The word 'and' here shows continuity with the previous stanza where the Cloud is depicted as about to address the Yakśiṇi.

[111] This is because the Cloud was performing a commendable act.

[112] The Yakśiṇi is referred to.

[113] The Yakśa is the narrator alluding to his wife, the Yakśiṇi.

[114] Here the 'Yakśa is indicated'.

Of those creatures,
Fallen victims to calamities,[115]
As a matter of course"

अङ्गेनाङ्गं प्रतनु तनुना गाढतप्तेन तप्तं
सास्त्रेणाश्रुद्रुतमविरतोत्कण्ठमुत्कण्ठितेन ।
उष्णोच्छ्वासं समधिकतरोच्छ्वासिना दूरवर्ती
संकल्पैस्तैर्विशति विधिना वैरिणा रुद्धमार्गः ॥४२॥

Verse No. 42:
"(The Yakśa with frame) much emaciated[116],
(His) path blocked by hostile fate,
Exceedingly feverish (out of passion),
Tearful out of longing,
Sighing excessively,
Far away (from his beloved);
By these longings[117],
(Seeking) to enter bodily,
The person (of his beloved),
Highly emaciated and feverish,
Wet with tears,
Being perpetually anxious,
(Emitting) hot sighs"

शब्दाख्येयं यदपि किल ते यः सखीनां पुरस्तात्,
कर्णे लोलः कथयितुमभूदाननस्पर्शलोभात् ।
सोऽतिक्रान्तः श्रवणविषयं लोचनाभ्यामदृश्य-
स्त्वामुत्कण्ठाविरचितपदं मन्मुखेनेदमाह ॥४३॥

---

[115] This is meant for the Yakśiṇi who needlessly had to undergo the ordeal of separation.
[116] This stanza is in continuation of the preceding stanza in which the Yakśa had begun to narrate his message to be conveyed by the Cloud to the Yakśiṇi. In this stanza the Yakśa wants his wife to know how desperate he is for a union with her, even if only in thoughts.
[117] The reference is Yakśa's yearnings for a union even though only mentally with his wife.

Verse No. 43:

"(In continuation of Yakśa's message to Yakśiṇī),
Though suitable indeed were the words,
For utterance in front of
Your (Yakśiṇī's) friends,
He[118] became eager,
To murmur (them) in (your)[119] ear,
Out of longing,
For touch of (your)[120] face,
Such a (very) one[121],
Being beyond the range of (your)[122] hearing,
(And) beyond the ken of (your)[123] vision,
Has conveyed to you[124] through me[125],
This verse strung together,
Out of (his)[126] longing (for you)"

श्यामास्वङ्गं चकितहरिणीप्रेक्षणे दृष्टिपातं
वक्त्रच्छायां शशिनि शिखिनां बर्हभारेषु केशान् ।
उत्पश्यामि प्रतनुषु नदीवीचिषु भ्रूविलासान्,
हन्तैकस्मिन् क्वचिदपि न ते चण्डि सादृश्यमस्ति ।।४४।।

Verse No. 44:

"I[127] deem it possible to discern,
In 'Priyangu' vines,
(Your)[128] (slim) figure;
In the glances of a bewildered doe,
(Your)[129] glances being cast down;

---

118 Alludes to Yakśa.
119 Alludes to the Yakśiṇi.
120 --ibid--
121 Connotes the Yakśa.
122 Alludes to the Yakśiṇi
123 --ibid--
124 --ibid--
125 Connotes the Cloud
126 Refers to the Yakśa.
127 Refers to the Yakśa.
128 The Yakśiṇi is meant.
129 --ibid--

In the moon,
The radiance of (your)[130] visage;
In the plumage of peacocks,
(Your)[131] hair;
In the gentle ripples of river,
Alluring movements of (your)[132] eyebrows;
But alas !
Oh ! one displaying mock wrathfulness! [133]
Nowhere even in one of them,
Is your resemblance[134]"

त्वामालिख्य प्रणयकुपितां धातुरागैः शिलाया-
मात्मानं ते चरणपतितं यावदिच्छामि कर्तुम् ।
अस्रैस्तावन्मुहुरुपचितैर्दृष्टिरालुप्यते मे
क्रूरस्तस्मिन्नपि न सहते सङ्गमं नौ कृतान्तः ।।४५।।

Verse No. 45:

"On a stone slab,
By mineral dyes,
Having painted yourself[135],
Displaying (mock) anger,
Arising out of (your) love (of me)[136];
Whenever I[137] seek to portray myself,
As fallen at your[138] feet,
Again and again then only my vision gets clouded,
By profusion of tears,

---

[130] --ibid--
[131] --ibid--
[132] --ibid--
[133] --ibid-- The Yakśa was fearful that he had offended his wife by seeking to discern her resemblance in this object or that. Hence he calls her Chandi or one making a show of anger playfully.
[134] The Yakśa then immediately tries to mollify his wife by saying there was none like her.
[135] Refers to the Yakśiṇi.
[136] As described in the earlier stanza, the Yakśiṇi was much offended, as per Yakśa's imagination because of his attempt to detect her resemblance in the surrounding world.
[137] Here the Yakśa is referred to.
[138] The Yakśiṇi is meant.

(Making that impossible);
Cruel fate not tolerating,
Our union,
Even if it were in that (painting) only"

मामाकाशप्रणिहितभुजं निर्दयाश्लेषहेतो-
लर्ब्धायास्ते कथमपि मया स्वप्नसंदर्शनेषु ।
पश्यन्तीनां न खलु बहुशो न स्थलीदेवतानां
मुक्तास्थूलास्तरुकिसलयेष्वश्रुलेशाः पतन्ति ।।४६।।

Verse No. 46:

"Somehow or other in a dream vision,
Myself[139] having got hold of you[140],
With a view to tightly embracing you;
Forest deities observing me[141],
Arms extended in space,
Usually (then) come down as a matter of course,
(Their) tear drops, large (like) pearls,
On plant leaves"

भित्त्वा सद्यः किसलयपुटान् देवदारुद्रुमाणां
ये तत्क्षीरस्रुतिसुरभयो दक्षिणेन प्रवृत्ताः ।
आलिङ्ग्यन्ते गुणवति मया ते तुषाराद्रिवाताः,
पूर्वं स्पृष्टं यदि किल भवेदङ्गमेभिस्तवेति ।।४७।।

Verse No. 47:

"These Himālayan winds blowing southwards,
Which having ripped open at once,
Bunched leaves of Devadāru trees,
Milk streaming thereof,
Scenting them;
Oh ! Virtuous one[142]

[139] Refers to the Yakśa. He continues to narrate his message meant for his wife to the Cloud.
[140] This connotes the Yakśiṇi.
[141] The Yakśa is referred.
[142] Reference to the Yakśiṇi.

By me they are embraced,
As in all likelihood,
Your body would have been touched,
Earlier by them"[143]

संक्षिप्येत क्षण इव कथं दीर्घयामा त्रियामा,
सर्वावस्थास्वहरपि कथं मन्दमन्दातपं स्यात् ।
इत्थं चेतश्चटुलनयने दुर्लभप्रार्थनं मे
गाढोष्माभिः कृतमशरणं त्वद्वियोगव्यथाभिः ॥४८॥

Verse No. 48:
"How could the (dark) night[144],
Never-ending being its hours,
Reduced to as if a moment;
How would the (agonizing) day,
Whatsoever be the conditions,
Turn out also to be the one,
Hardly of any warmth;
Oh ! the one with tremulous eyes,
Such being the entreaty,
Hard of fulfilment,[145]
In my mind,
Rendered helpless,
By pangs of separation,
From you,
Deeply perturbing"

नन्वात्मानं बहु विगणयन्नात्मनैवावलम्बे,
तत्कल्याणि ! त्वमपि नितरां मा गमः कातरत्वम् ।
कस्यात्यन्तं सुखमुपनतं दुःखमेकान्ततो वा,

---

[143] The Mahākavi thus expresses Yakśa's overwhelming love of the Yakśiṇi. This is in continuation of his message to the Cloud to be conveyed to the Yakśiṇi.

[144] In continuation of the last few stanzas in which the Yakśa conveys his message to his wife.

[145] The Yakśa was desperate to unite at once with his beloved wife. But this was impossible as he was cursed to be away from her.

नीचैर्गच्छत्युपरि च दशा चक्रनेमिक्रमेण ।।४९।।

Verse No. 49:

"Oh ! my darling[146],
Pondering deeply,
(About my[147] miserable condition),
I[148] have sustained myself,
Only by my[149] (own exertions);
Therefore, oh ! benevolent one[150],
You too do not become,
Excessively agitated;
(In fact),
Who is there,
Who has obtained,
Either extreme happiness (for ever),
Or only sorrow after sorrow;
Up and down goes (indeed),
The state of (an individual)[151],
(Like) the rotating rim of a wheel"

शापान्तो मे भुजगशयनादुत्थिते शार्ङ्गपाणौ
शेषान्मासान् गमय चतुरो लोचने मीलयित्वा ।
पश्चादावां विरहगुणितं तं तमात्माभिलाषं
निर्वेक्ष्यावः परिणतशरच्चन्द्रिकासु क्षपासु ।।५०।।

Verse No. 50:

"With the rising of (Bhagawan Viṣnu)[152],
The holder of horny bow,
From the serpent - couch,

---

146 Refers to the Yakśiṇi.
147 Refers to the Yakśa.
148 --ibid--
149 --ibid--
150 Refers to the Yakśiṇi.
151 In the Mahākavi's writings one often comes across the theme that the man's fortune keeps on changing like a turning wheel.
152 This was to occur during the next Kārtikka Śukla Ekadaśi which was then four months away.

Will be the termination,
Of my[153] curse;
Spend[154] (thus) the remaining four months,
Ignoring everything (keeping eyes closed);
We will then,
During the autumnal nights of perfect moonlight,
Fulfil each and every of our craving,
As thought of,
During the (period) of separation"

भूयश्चाह त्वमपि शयने कण्ठलग्ना पुरा मे
निद्रां गत्वा किमपि रुदती सस्वनं विप्रबुद्धा ।
सान्तर्हासं कथितमसकृत् पृच्छतश्च त्वया मे,
दृष्टः स्वप्ने कितव ! रमयन् कामपि त्वं मयेति ।।५१।।

Verse No. 51:

"And again (the Yakśa) said,
(Addressing the Yakśiṇī),
In the days of yore,
Though asleep on the bed,
Clinging to my[155] neck,
You[156] (suddenly) woke up,
Crying aloud for some reason whatever;
And (after) my[157] questioning again and again,
(As to why this),
With a repressed smile,
By you[158] was conveyed,
Oh ! rogue ! seen in a dream by me[159],
Were you,[160]
Frolicking with a damsel"

---

[153] This refers to the Yakśa. Eight months of the curse period had already elapsed.
[154] Exhortation of the Yakśa to the Yakśiṇi.
[155] Refers to the Yakśa.
[156] Refers to the Yakśiṇi.
[157] --ibid--155
[158] Refers to the Yakśiṇi.
[159] --ibid--
[160] Refers to the Yakśa.

एतस्मान्मां कुशलिनमभिज्ञानदानाद् विदित्वा
मा कौलीनादसितनयने मय्यविश्वासिनी भूः ।
स्नेहानाहुः किमपि विरहे ध्वंसिनस्ते त्वभोगा-
दिष्टे वस्तुन्युपचितरसाः प्रेमराशीभवन्ति ।।५२।।

Verse No. 52:

"(In this way),[161]
Having been given this proof,
Identifying (me)[162],
(As the sender of this message);
(And also) being aware of
my[163] well-being (now),
Oh ! black-eyed one[164],
Do not become the one,
Due to vicious rumour mongering,
Bereft of faith in me,
(As to myself being no more alive);
During separation they say,
Somehow or other,
(Bonds) of love are liable to disintegrate;
But due to non-fulfilment,
They turn into,
Heaps of love,
With the objects of desire,
Overflowing with sweetness"

आश्वास्यैवं प्रथमविरहोदग्रशोकां सखीं ते
शैलादाशु त्रिनयनवृषोत्खातकूटान्निवृत्तः ।
साभिज्ञानप्रहितकुशलैस्तद्वचोभिर्ममाऽपि,
प्रातः कुन्दप्रसवशिथिलं जीवितं धारयेथाः ।।५३।।

---

[161] By narration of a highly intimate episode from the personal life of the Yakśa and Yakśiṇi.
[162] Refers to Yakśa.
[163] --Ibid--
[164] Connotes the Yakśiṇi.

Verse No. 53:

"In this way,[165]
Having reassured your friend,[166]
(Immersed) in deep sorrow due to separation,
For the first time (from me, the Yakśa);
Having (then) returned forthwith,
From the (Kailaś) mountain,
Its peak dug up,
(By the horns) of the bull,
Of Śivaji (the three-eyed God);
(Returning) along with the memento (sent) (by the Yakśiṇi),
As well as the words conveying (her) well-being;
Protect (thus) my life also,
Feeble (like) a Kunda flower,
Early in the morning"

कच्चित् सौम्य व्यवसितमिदं बन्धुकृत्यं त्वया मे
प्रत्यादेशान्न खलु भवतो धीरतां कल्पयामि ।
निःशब्दोऽपि प्रदिशसि जलं याचितश्चातकेभ्यः
प्रत्युक्तं हि प्रणयिषु सतामीप्सितार्थक्रियैव ।।५४।।

Verse No. 54:

"Oh ! gentle one,[167]
Surely this task[168] (of your) brother,[169]
Of myself,[170]
Be performed by you,[171]
Won't it;
I cannot possibly imagine,
The (silent) gravitas of your honour[172],

---

[165] In the previous two verses (no. 51 and 52) the Cloud had provided the Yakśiṇi with a convincing proof that the Yakśa was alive.

[166] The Cloud is Yakśa's friend. The Yakśiṇi is therefore described as the Cloud's friend or 'your friend'.

[167] The Yakśa here is addressing the Cloud.

[168] Of delivering the message.

[169] Here Yakśa is referred to.

[170] --ibid--

[171] The Cloud is connoted.

As a rejection,
(Of my entreaty[173]);
You provide water,
Having been implored,
To Chātaka[174] birds,
Though being wordless;
Verily the response of the righteous,
To the (prayers) of supplicants,
Is nothing but,
Carrying out what is desired[175]"

एतत्कृत्वा प्रियमनुचितप्रार्थनावर्तिनो मे
सौहर्दाद् वा विधुर इति वा मय्यनुक्रोशबुद्ध्या ।
इष्टान् देशान् जलद ! विचर प्रावृषा संभृतश्री–
र्मा भूदेवं क्षणमपि च ते विद्युता विप्रयोगः ।।५५।।

Verse No. 55:
"Either out of friendship,
Or sense of pity for me,[176]
Being separated (from the beloved),
Having accomplished this (mission),[177]
Dear to me,
(Despite) myself putting forth an improper solicitation;[178]
Wander off, Oh ! Cloud,
Over wonderful regions,
(Your) glory enhanced by the rainy season;
And may there not be,

---

[172] --ibid--
[173] This is to convey Yakśa's message.
[174] This is a mythical bird commonly referred to in the Sanskrit literature. It partakes of rain water only as it falls.
[175] The basic purport of this stanza is as follows. The Cloud could not give for obvious reasons an audible affirmative response to Yakśa's entreaty. But the Yakśa does not take it as a refusal, pointing out that the clouds fulfil the needs of Chātaka birds entreating for water, though remaining silent.
[176] Refers to the Yakśa.
[177] Connotes the cloud successfully delivering the Yakśa's message to his wife.
[178] As explained in stanza no. 5 in the Purvardh the Cloud was hardly regarded as an appropriate messenger for carrying the message of love.

Even momentarily your separation,
From the lightning,
Like this,
(As happened in my case)[179] "

[179] The lightning and the Cloud are deemed as the eternal pair of lovers. Yakśa evidently did not want the Cloud to suffer from pangs of separation even momentarily as he had done.

Brief note about the Author

Dr. Prakash Joshi joined the Indian Foreign Service in early 1970s.He went on to hold various senior positions with distinction in different parts of the world, including the Gulf region, Africa, Europe, the Caribbean, etc. While posted to Guyana,South America, as High Commissioner, he delivered on their TV network discourses on the Gita for over two years.

The author was educated in Cambridge, Gonville and Caius College, U.K. where he did Tripos in Mathematics. He had earlier graduated with high honours from the University of Bombay specializing in Mathematics. He was then nominated as a National Scholar and was awarded the prestigious Tata Scholarship for higher Education for Indians. During 1980s while posted in Delhi he completed his doctorate through the Jawaharlal Nehru University in the field of International Relations. He also qualified at that time as Interpreter in Arabic through the School of Foreign Languages, New Delhi. The author possesses excellent knowledge of Sanskrit. Dr. Joshi has a distinguished family background and his father Dr. V.M. Joshi, I.C.S., D.Sc. was a renowned statistician.

Dr. Prakash Joshi has several publications to his credit in the field of Hindu metaphysics. These include

1) Saga of Hinduism-Volumes I and II: M. D. Publications, New Delhi.

2) Introduction to Sankara'sAdvaitism: Motilal Banarasidass Publishers, New Delhi. Revised Edition published by Motilal Banarsidass International, Delhi.

3) Path to Liberation from known to unknown: Motilal Banarasidass Publishers, New Delhi. Revised edition published by Motilal Banarsidass International, Delhi.

4) From Vedanta to Modern Science: Ocean Books Pvt. Ltd. New Delhi.

5) Present Day Gita - a way of Life: Publisher K. G. Ganju, New Delhi. Revised edition is under publication with Motilal Banarsidass International, Delhi.

6) The Golden Decade 2005-2015, My life as Hony Consul General : Publisher: K. G. Ganju,New Delhi

7) Quest: My spiritual journey - in search of happiness, Volumes I & II by Motilal Banarsidass International, Delhi (under publication).

The author is also engaged in systematically translating Sanskrit classics into English. His published works are:

8) Translation of Shākuntalam: Publisher: Somanath Sanskrit University

9) Translation of MudrāRākshasam: Publisher: Somanath Sanskrit University

Forthcoming translations of the author of Sanskrit Classics into English with extensive footnotes:

10) Mālvikāgnimitram.

11) Vikramorvaśīyam

12) ZtusaAhāra

Other future publications of the author:

13) Translation into English of Sundarkānd.

14) How to beat the calculator -have fun with numbers the Vedic way.

15) A concise commentary on the Gita: original verses with transliteration. Extensive quotations from Gyāneshwari and Sri SriParamahansaYogānanda.

16) Main themes of the Gita - its essence: original verses with transliteration.